SHADOW OF THE TRAITOR

CHILDREN OF THE CURSED SERIES BOOK 2

A.E. STANFILL

Published 2020 by Shadow City – A Next Chapter Imprint

Cover art by CoverMint

CHAPTER ONE

A SHIP AT SEA

Storm clouds were rolling in, a once blue and calm sky now darkened by those very clouds. Huge waves of ocean water crashed hard into the only ship that was brave enough to battle the storm itself. Lightning filled the sky in all different patterns. The wind picked up and the waves grew larger, damn near causing the ship to steer off course. If the storm gets any worse it will threaten to capsize the vessel.

"Lower the mass!" A voice shouted.

"Not sure if that is possible in such a storm such as this!"

"Where is the Captain?" Another shouted.

"He's below deck dealing with the prisoners."

"The Captain has had them alive for over a year and still nothing. It would be better if we just collected the reward."

"It would be unwise to question him at this point."

"Then I guess we better make sure the ship doesn't sink."

Down below the Captain of the vessel was with the thieves executioner. Wishing to inquire some information from his new found guests. "Tell me, Aurelius. Why does the new King Drasal have such a high bounty on your friends' heads?" The Captain asked.

"I wouldn't tell you a damn thing!" Aurelius spate. "Even if you threatened to cut out my tongue."

"Why would I do that to an old friend?"

"You are no friend of mine."

The man laughed, "That hurts. How long have we known one another?"

"Many years. Perhaps not long enough though, Bosch."

Bosch walked closer to the cell door, he was safe as long as he kept his distance. "All I want out of you is information, then you will be free to do as you please," he said.

"And what of my friends?"

"Like it or not. They are the property of Kole now."

"If I refuse?"

"I will be forced to let my new acquaintance here have some alone time with you."

"Do you think that scares me?"

"I would assume it wouldn't," Bosch said. "That's why I brought a friend along with me. Executioner, bring me the boy." A moment later the overly large man returned with a young man that had shoulder length blonde hair. He was somewhat muscular and was dressed in ragged clothing the same as Aurelius. "I see by the look in your eyes that you thought this boy would be elsewhere," he smirked.

"Leave him alone he has nothing to do with this!" Aurelius demanded.

"He has everything to do with this!" Bosch shouted back. "Tell me why King Alistair wants this child so badly and no harm shall come to him."

"Don't tell this scum anything," said the young man.

Captain Bosch backhanded him across the face, "I did not give you permission to speak. Still your tongue if you wish it to stay in your mouth." He turned his attention back to Aurelius, "What do you say old friend? Do you wish to talk with me now?"

"Damn you, Bosch." He turned his back towards him refusing to say another word.

"I don't think you believe me. Let's see if you will speak after this. Cut off the boys thumb, then throw it in the cell with my old friend here. Teach him a lesson about respecting the captain of the ship."

"Leave him be! You have no idea the consequences if you persist!"

The executioner grabbed hold of the young man's wrist slamming his hand against the wall. He removed his knife from the sheath of leather attached to his belt. Pressing the blade against the flesh of the boys thumb readying to cut it right off.

"One last chance. What do you say, Aurelius?"

"Leave the boy alone and I will tell you whatever you want to know." But it was too late, the young man was already losing control of his senses. Which allowed whatever power that dwells deep within him to escape. Blue flames erupted from his hand, his strength increased enough that the executioner could barely keep hold of the boy.

"What kind of sorcery is this?" Bosch gasped.

"I warned you," Aurelius said. "Whatever comes next is of your own doing."

The executioner went to stab the young man but quickly realized he no longer had the knife in hand. Instead the young man had the weapon, before he could react the blade cut through his wrist. He watched in disbelief as his hand dropped to the floor. The man fell to the ground crying out in pain, grasping at what was no longer there. Bosch went for his blade but the boy was already upon him with the knife at his throat.

"Leon stop!" Aurelius shouted. Though his words were not getting through to him as Leon pressed the knife into his flesh. "If you kill him we will never know where he took Gawain and the others!"

"How can you trust he will tell us the truth?" Leon questioned.

"Throw me the keys he carries and I will show you how."

"If you move an inch you die," Leon warned, reaching out to take the keys from the man's belt. He turned ever so slightly tossing the set of keys over to Aurelius. The elven man reached down and picked them up, going through each key until he found the one that unlocked the cell door.

"You okay, Leon?" Aurelius asked as he rejoined one of his companions.

"Hungry and thirsty, other than that I'm alright," Leon answered. "You?"

"Same."

"You will never get away with this, my men will kill you before you get topside," Bosch interrupted.

"If you don't help us you will lose the one thing you love the most," Aurelius said.

"Do you think I care that much for my own life?" Bosch laughed.

"Shut up!" Leon snapped.

"Bosch is right, his life matters not to him," Aurelius said. "But there is one thing that he does care for and is afraid of losing."

"Do tell. Let's find out if you know me as well as you think you do."

Aurelius muttered a few elven words under his breath. Seconds later a silver sphere appeared in the palm of his left hand. "You see this old friend?" He asked with a slight grin. "This sphere allows me to control the weather when out at sea. And while you've been down here with us, I've been controlling the weather up there."

"What's your point?"

"My point is that I have been building a storm that not even your ship can survive."

"You would sink the, Dauntless?"

"If you sink the ship you will kill us all," Leon gasped.

"Don't worry about that," said Aurelius. "The Good Captain will announce to his crew that he had a change of heart. That we would be a better use to him as an alliance than an enemy."

"Why would I do that?"

Aurelius shrugged, "If you don't then Leon will slit your throat and I will be forced to sink your ship. I will leave that choice to you, Captain."

Captain Bosch thought about his choices, die and lose his ship in the process. Or let his prisoners that he was being paid handsomely to transport to King Alistair himself go. Though the thought of his ship being sunk along with him on it wasn't something he was willing to allow so easily. That and if his ship was gone so would be all of his riches. Along with what he loved the most, adventure and plundering other pirate ships.

"Looks like the shoe is on the other foot." Bosch laughed, "Call off the boy and stop the storm and you have a deal."

Aurelius took the knife from Leon and held it up to Bosch's throat himself, reconsidering the deal that was made. "I should kill you for selling me and my friends out."

"Then you will never know where I've taken the rest of your mates." Bosch smiled. Aurelius lowered the blade afterwards punching him in the face. Bosch wiped the blood from his lips, "Still got that elven temper I see."

"Shut up," Aurelius hissed. "Leon, go get our gear."

About thirty minutes later the Captain emerged from below deck, his second in command was happy to see his return. "Captain Bosch! Thank the gods you are safe, these waters be cursed. We fought a mighty storm, then it disappeared as quickly as it started," he stated.

"Steady your nerve mate," Bosch said. "We have been in cursed waters before and shall again. If my second in command can not handle this job anymore. Maybe walking the plank is more suitable for thee."

"No need for that Captain," he nervously swallowed. That's when he spotted the prisoners walking up topside. "Why have the prisoners been set free?"

"I have decided they will be more valuable to me as allies rather than enemies."

"Surely delivering them to King Alistair would garner us loyalty. Would it not?"

"Do you question my decision?!" Bosch belted.

"Not at all sir."

"Then stay your tongue before I cut it out."

"As you wish Captain." The man bowed before quickly walking away.

"About our destination, Captain," Aurelius began.

"Just call me, Bosch." He sighed.

"Can't take that chance," said Aurelius. "If we don't pretend to show you respect your crew could decide to mutiny. And neither one of us can afford for that to happen."

"True, and knowing my crew they would surely throw us overboard," he said. "Where to then?"

"Take us to where Master Gawain and the rest of my friends are," Leon insisted.

"That will not be so easy," Bosch replied.

"Why?" Aurelius asked.

"I bought them from Kole then sold your friends off to slave traders at Wintervale."

"Even though you were supposed to take them all back to Drasal," said Aurelius. "How did you get away with trying such a scheme?"

"I sent a messenger to Drasal, informing King Alistair the prisoners tried to escape and there had been casualties. Only the boy with the blonde hair was left alive."

"Smart, even for you."

"More silver in it for me that way."

Aurelius shook his head, "If you don't mind Captain we would like to go to Wintervale."

"Listen up!" Bosch shouted. "Hoist the mainsail we head for the great frozen city of Wintervale!"

Five days of rough waters and battling storms that for some reason the sphere Aurelius carried couldn't control. Almost as if the gods themselves were against them. Finally made landfall or had gotten as close as they possibly could before having to take out a dinghy. Though Bosch tried to give his word he wouldn't leave. He still couldn't be trusted and was forced by Aurelius and Leon to come with to ensure they had a way off this dreadful place.

It was cold, colder than most places Leon had visited before. Aurelius was used to such changes in temperatures as he had traveled far and wide. All three of them were dressed in heavy coats made from the fur of the Wintervale wolf. Which holds special abilities to protect man from such frigid weather. That and the little food that was with them was enough to keep them alive. This was all new to Leon, never had he seen land such as this. Nothing but a frozen tundra, not much in the way of wildlife and trees that were iced over.

After a long and dangerous hike through snow and below freezing temperatures that took three days. They had finally made it to their destination. Walking into the city for Leon was strange and made his stomach crawl. Yes he was a stranger in a strange and foreign land. Though seeing houses made from ice and vendors selling their wares near small contained fires was not something he was used to seeing. First thought that came to mind was the simple fact of how people could survive in this manor?

"Take us to where you sold Gawain and the others," Aurelius demanded.

"It won't be that easy," replied Bosch.

"What are you not telling us?"

"I sold them to a group of mercenaries that have a base in this city."

"Mercenaries?" Leon interrupted. "How in the hell are we going to get them back from a group of scum such as that?"

"Everyone has a price," Aurelius reassured him. "Isn't that right, Bosch?"

"I don't like that look in your eyes."

"You're going to offer to buy Gawain and the others back, even if you have to offer double the coin."

"Are you mad?"

"Do you wish to keep your life intact?"

Bosch sighed, "These men may wish for something more."

"Whatever it takes," Aurelius proclaimed.

"Remember you said that."

"Let me worry about that. Lead the way towards their base."

The Captain did as he was told, knowing if he didn't his life and his precious ship would be done for. The mercenary camp was on the far side of town. There was at least five medium size tents surrounding one large tent dead in the center. As they approached, there were groups of men on both sides practicing combat techniques. One man in particular caught the attention of Aurelius and Leon. The way he moved, the combat techniques he used, his defensive stance seemed all too familiar.

"It's, Master Gawain," Leon said out of the blue.

Aurelius was thinking the same but had second thoughts after seeing the man's scruffy looks. "How can you be sure?" He asked. "Yes he fights the same as, Gawain. But let's be honest, he would never allow himself to look like that."

"Not sure if you've noticed but neither one of us is looking great either." Leon retorted.

"Why would he teach a bunch of swords for hire the knowledge he learned from the Academy?" Aurelius asked. "Do you not question that?"

"That does bother me," Leon answered. "Though Gawain has trained me since I was a mere child. So don't question me when I say that man is none other than Master Gawain."

Aurelius only knew of one way to get Gawain's attention if it was truly him. It was a game of one-upmanship that the two played every time they would meet in a different location. He focused his concentration on directing a spell of ice towards the palm of his hand. When done he reared back and threw a large ice crystal at the man Leon believed to be Master Gawain.

The man turned and released a spell of fire to melt the ice crystal before it could hit him. "Only one man would try a stunt like that!" He bellowed.

"Gawain, that is you!" Aurelius shouted in return.

"Aurelius, Leon! Thank the gods you two are safe," Gawain proclaimed. He walked over to happily greet them both. "I worried the worst for you both." Gawain was ecstatic until he had seen the monster that sold him and Lady Catherine. Along with the two other boys to the mercenaries. "Scum!" He said with rage filling his voice. "You sold us out to Kole, this man will die by my hand!"

Gawain went to reach for his blade but Aurelius was quick to stop him. "Steady yourself, we need him alive if we are to leave this land."

"I would rather gut him like a pig for what he has done!"

"Believe me, I would like nothing more than to see that happen. But at this moment in time we need him alive."

"Because you wish to spare his life so be it." Gawain glanced over at Bosch, "When there is no further use for you, then you shall answer for your crimes."

"I look forward to our one on one time," Bosch replied with a slight smile on his face.

"Master Gawain, why are you training a band of mercenaries?" Leon questioned.

"That is a long story," Gawain replied. "And please do not refer to me as Master. That is a title that is no longer mine to claim."

"Either way we are here to get you and the others out of here." Aurelius proclaimed.

"What if I refuse?" Gawain asked.

"Why would you do such a thing?"

"Walk with me as we talk," Gawain turned and slowly walked ahead with the others following suit. "Not that you two could understand what has transpired over the past two years. But I have found myself in a fortunate position." A man came running up to him wearing clad armor. He handed over a piece of parchment and they exchanged a few words before the man took his leave.

"What is going on here?" Aurelius questioned.

Gawain proceeded to walk, "As I was saying, I found myself in a fortunate position. When myself and the others were sold to this band of mercenaries. I thought for sure we would be nothing more than slaves, lucky for us that wasn't the case.

The leader of this band of mercenaries was a kind man that refused to let us be sold to slave traders. He led that traitorous scum to believe he had cruel intentions in mind for us. It was in fact the only way he would allow us to be sold in the first place-"

"Couldn't have cared less what would have happened to the lot of you," Bosch interrupted. "Coin was the thing that I wanted out of you. Hell, I would have sold you to Hades himself if the price was right."

"Filthy swine," Gawain muttered.

"You still have yet to answer my question," said Aurelius.

"After Mace Smith, whom I learned a lot from over the past couple of years, had passed away. I stepped in as their new leader, these are my men now, my family, this is my home," Gawain explained.

"Have you lost your mind?"

"Far from it. Ask the others when you see them, I assure you they feel the same way."

Leon sighed, "What of our quest?"

Gawain stopped to face the young man, "What chance would we have against King Alistair and that damned blade?" He lowered his head almost as if he felt shameful, "I let Ulrich and you down, Leon. Most of all, I let the Academy down, for that people paid with their lives. Because of me Alistair became King and now controls the most powerful blade in all the lands."

"Though the tide will turn in our favor once we go to The Tomb Of Carnage!" Leon proclaimed.

"You know this from a dream!" Gawain shouted. "This means nothing! He who holds the Reaper Blade controls the Dark Knights. How do we stand a chance against such power? And you talk about some amulet and tomb that will lead us to victory. It is a waste of time, we need to get as far away as we can and start anew."

"You would allow more innocent to die?"

"I refuse to let more people that I care about die!"

Leon glared at Gawain, "When did you become a coward?" He muttered under his breath.

"What did you say to me child?" Gawain hissed.

The young man clenched his fists together tight, his eyes opened wide and his upper lip snarled as he spoke, "I said, when does the Master Trainer of the Academy of Drasel act as though a coward."

Gawain took a step forward, "I am no coward. Remember who you speak too," he warned. Leon held back his anger out of respect for the man he still considered a brother. If his words did come forth a fight would break out and that was not what was needed at this time. The young man stormed past Gawain and quickly disappeared out of sight.

"What has happened to you, Gawain?" Aurelius asked.

"I've opened my eyes to the truth," Gawain replied. "Follow me, I have matters to attend too. After that we can talk further."

"What of, Leon?"

"Leave him be," said Gawain. "He has to grow up sooner or later."

CHAPTER TWO

OLD FRIENDS AND OLD PROBLEMS

Leon was looking the city over if that is what one would like to call it. There were many huts all around, nothing like what he was used to seeing. Not much in the way of coin around these parts of the lands, hunting for fur and meat was the only means to survival. Yes there were traders selling their wares but they were few and far between. Though there was no castle to be seen. Which meant no one person had power or control over the city of ice.

"Leon!" A voice called out.

When he turned to look, he saw an old friend waving at him, "Henry!" Leon shouted back.

"It's damn good to see you, Leon," Henry said as he approached. "Thought for sure you would be dead or worse in prison being torchered by King Alistair's lackeys, Cain and Ulrich."

Leon laughed at the notion, "No such luck," he said. "Though I would like another chance to speak with Ulrich."

It looked as though Henry's chin was about to hit the ground, "Why in the hell would you want to talk with that scum for?" He spate.

"His mind is being poisoned by, Caine. You know what Ulrich was like well before I came to the Academy. He would never raise a hand towards anyone."

"Maybe he was once kind, but not anymore. Or perhaps he never was in the first place."

"How can you talk that way about our friend?"

"That coward is no friend of mine!"

Leon was quick to change the subject, it had been over two years since he had seen them last. Having an argument was the last thing he wanted, "Where's Jeffrey and Lady Catherine?"

"Jeffrey, is out hunting," he said. "Lady Catherine, is teaching healing techniques at the hut up ahead on your right."

"Has everyone lost their minds?"

"We found a home, Leon," Henry answered. "A home away from the troubles that plague the world. Nobody cares about a town that is made from ice. We can live here in peace with no worries, help the ones that need and deserve it."

"And what of the ones that can't escape that tyrant?" Leon shouted. "Do we just leave the rest of the world suffer?"

"What do you suggest?"

"We fight!"

Henry laughed, "I think you're the one that is mad," he said. "You can't fight someone that powerful."

Leon raised his head high, "I can," he said with pride.

"Last time you went up against Alistair he almost killed you."

"This time will be different!"

"How can you be so sure?"

"You will just have to trust me."

Henry sighed, "Don't look for my help. You might be able to get aid from the others, but I'm done fighting. My home is here," he said. The young man slapped Leon on the shoulder, "Go talk with Lady Catherine, I'm sure she will be happy to see you well." Henry smiled before turning to walk away.

Leon couldn't believe what he was hearing, first Gawain refusing to hear him out, then Henry after that. Perhaps Lady Catherine still had a level head on her shoulders. He could only hope that would be the case, she may be the only one left to help talk sense into Gawain and Henry. When he walked into the hut Lady Catherine was in the middle of teaching a class on healing herbs and remedies.

Though she stopped everything when she caught a glimpse of Leon standing off in the distance. "Class is dismissed for the day," she announced. When the small hut was cleared out Lady Catherine approached. "Leon," she gasped before hugging him. "By the Gods I thought the worst had happened."

"Likewise," Leon replied.

"How did you escape?"

"Long story."

She hugged him again, "Doesn't matter, you're here, you're safe."

Leon took a step back, "I don't think I can handle another hug." He smiled, "But I'm glad to see you again, Lady Catherine."

"The Academy no longer exists," Catherine responded. "That title no longer belongs to me."

"Gawain said the same. Then what shall I call you?"

"Hmm." She tapped the tip of her finger on her lips, "I give you permission to call me, Catherine."

"It will take some getting used to," he said. "Though I will try."

Catherine noticed that something else was bothering the young man, "You seemed troubled, Leon. Just as before, feel free to speak about whatever is on your mind," she reassured him.

"It's about Master Gawain."

"What about him?"

"He's changed."

"Gawain seems the same to me."

"Then why is he afraid to finish what we started?"

"He's not afraid."

"If it's not fear what is it?" Leon questioned.

She placed her hands on Leon's shoulders and looked him straight in the eyes, "He's lost himself," she answered. "Everything he has known, loved and protected was taken from him in a blink of an eye. Deep down he feels like he let everyone down, including you."

"What can I do to help him snap out of it?"

"I'm afraid I can't help you with that."

"Why not?"

"That is something he will have to deal with in time."

"I need the old Gawain back now!" Leon shouted.

"Do not speak to me in such a manner," she demanded.

"I didn't mean it." He frowned, "I need his help and Gawain has refused. He has said that this is his home now and has no plans on leaving. Aurelius and myself can't do this alone and we desperately need to get to the Tomb Of Carnage."

"Gawain wishes not to go there," Catherine replied. "He expressed his concerns long ago."

"What did he say?"

She crossed her arms and gave a stern look, "The place is dangerous, it is filled with undead creatures. And if not careful the Tomb itself can come to life and swallow your soul," she explained.

"Nothing we haven't faced before," Leon said with arrogance.

"Yes that is true," Catherine responded. "Though there is one creature that dwells deep within the Tomb that you have yet to face. This creature is the protector of what lies deep within, The Tomb Of Carnage. No man has ever stepped foot inside and lived to tell the tale. Gawain knows this and feels as though if you enter he will not have the strength to protect you."

"It doesn't matter what awaits me inside that place, I have no choice but to go. It is the only way to unlock the power of this amulet I carry with me, and thus will aid us in stopping, Alistair."

"How would a child know such things?" Catherine questioned.

"I am no longer a child and refuse to be treated as such!" Leon belted.

Catherine chuckled slightly, "My apologies young one," she said. "Still, how would you know this is the location you must go too?"

"You will just have to trust in my words."

"There is no way I can just trust in your words, the course of action you're taking is far too dangerous. I need more than your words alone if I am to believe you."

Leon let out a sigh of frustration, he had to think of something quick. He couldn't tell her about how he traveled to different realms or of his cursed blood. Not even he was able to put everything together enough to grasp the situation at hand. The only thing he was sure of was Robin's words of the Tomb being the place he needed to head for. "The elven lady Allora spoke of the place to me. Said it would be of great aid to our quest if we are to stop, Alistair." Yes it was a lie but it was the only thing he could think of.

"And she told you this herself?"

"Indeed," he said. "She also said we had to be there when the wolf moon reaches the highest point in the sky."

"That is one year away," Catherine responded, her face twitching nervously.

"That is why we need to act with haste."

"Give me three days to talk with Gawain," she said. "You will have an answer by then.

"You will have until the morning," Leon retorted.

"That is not long enough."

"I am sorry Catherine, that is all the time I can spare. I shall speak with Aurelius tonight. If Gawain and the rest of you are not waiting for us at that time, I shall have my answer." Leon bowed to her before taking his leave.

Later that night Catherine would find Gawain outside near a campfire looking up at the stars. He was deep in thought and had a troubled look on his face. She walked up and joined him by the fire. Gawain had no idea she was there until she took his hand in hers. Gawain looked over at her and offered a half hearted smile.

"Fancy meeting you here," Catherine said with a smile.

"You say that every time," Gawain replied.

"Like all the times before I'm guessing you have something on your mind."

"You know me all too well."

"Tell me. What troubles you?"

Gawain looked back up at the night sky, the clouds had covered the stars and snow began to fall like so many times before. "Leon and Aurelius need my help, though I fear that wouldn't be a wise choice," he answered.

Her gaze shifted to his face, "And why is that?" she asked. When he didn't look at her or give a response. She reached up and cupped his chin in her hand, pulling his gaze towards her. "Gawain, you're not answering me." She smiled.

Gawain frowned, "I failed the last time and people I cared for died. If it happens again the whole world will fall into chaos," he said.

"Don't forget that you made a promise to Leon's father and King Edward."

"Do you not think I know that!" He hissed. "If that child was to die then all hope for mankind would be over. We must keep him safe, that was the promise I had made."

"Remember, Leon is young and ambitious, he will go to the tomb with or without you. If you are there with him it's unlikely he will do something that will end his life. You know he is quick to act without thinking of the consequences."

"What if I don't have the strength?"

Catherine moved Gawain's hair out of his face, "You're the strongest person I know. Look around at what you have done for this town and its people. Not many can say they have accomplished what you have in so little time," she said. "Leon said they are leaving at sunrise if you choose to go meet them then. Looks like you have a choice to make." Cathrine kissed him on the cheek, "Goodnight, Gawain."

"Goodnight my lady." Gawain bowed. He watched until she disappeared into the darkness, leaving him alone with his thoughts. Not sure which path he should choose was weighing on him heavily. He wasn't one to break a promise even though both of those men were dead. And for some reason unbeknownst to him he was chosen by that damn blade he found to carry out this mission. There were choices he would have to make and not a lot of time to do so.

Aurelius and Leon awoke at first light, said their goodbyes and looked for Gawain. After they discovered he was nowhere to be found the group headed out of town. Leon was disappointed, but he must carry on with the task at hand with or without his old master. At the docking site where the dinghy awaited. A group of six seemed to be standing there waiting, perhaps to rob them of their goods and small boat. They cautiously approached with their blades drawn, though their chances of victory against such odds were slim to none.

Aurelius sheathed his blade and wiped the sweat from his forehead, "It is only Gawain and the others."

"Jeffrey is with them and so is Catherine!" Leon happily replied.

"Leon!" Jeffrey was shouting and waving.

"Jeffrey!" Leon shouted back.

"It's good to see that you came to your senses," Aurelius joked with Gawain. "What made you change your mind?"

Gawain shrugged, "I haven't changed my mind," he said. "We are in need of a vessel and yours will do just fine."

"What makes you believe you can accommodate ours?"

"You need my help right?"

"We're in need of your help, that much is true."

"Help me and my men with a job that needs to be done and we shall return the favor." Gawain crossed his arms and cracked a slight smile, "See where I'm going with this?"

"That's how you're going to play this?"

"It would seem so," Gawain said.

"You have changed over the years."

"The world changes along with the ones that inhabit it, all I've done is changed along with it."

It was more of a demand from an old friend than asking for a favor. Aurelius was glad that Leon was caught up talking to a friend of his own and not listening to a man he once called his teacher. But perhaps this deal could prove fruitful in a way. They would have Gawain back plus the aid of many strong armed men.

A day or two had passed while sailing the seas, and with Aurelius controlling the weather with his orb all was calm. Not only that, luck had been on their side as well with no signs of pirate ships or military vessels patrolling the waters.

As nerves were sitting in with Aurelius and Leon wishing to make haste to their destination. Gawain assured them both his mission would be quick and they could be on their way to the Tomb Of Carnage afterwards. Though he didn't tell them much of his mission, what they could gather is he was to transport a person of importance to another Kingdom. However something told them this mission wasn't going to be as quick and easy as Gawain claimed.

The sun was just starting to set, orange rays of light danced across the water. A show of the fact dusk had made its presence known to the travelers out at sea. All was calm and serene until the lookout from the crowsnest yelled out, "land ahead!" And with that Gawain looked over at the Captain to give the signal to dock at the port. Bosch gave the order to lower the main sails and ease into the dock as Gawain had wished.

Being as it was getting late, Gawain did not wish to show up for the mission at hand until bright and early the next day. On that night they would sleep yet again on the ship and depart at the break of dawn. Though Leon being the hard headed young man that he was. Decided to sneak off the ship and explore the Kingdom on his own.

Leon was astonished at the sheer size of the Kingdom, he had only seen so much of the world and this was new even to him. One thought crossed his mind that saddened him. His best friend of many years was not here to see such sights with him. Even though Ulrich had aligned himself with Caine and Alistair he was still Leon's friend no matter what. And he was bound and determined to convince Ulrich he was making a mistake next they meet.

But that was thoughts for another time and Leon shrugged it off for the time being to continue his search of the city. The young man slowly started to forget about the mission and began to have a little fun of his own. At the Captains expense of course, a few gold and silver coins Leon acquired from Bosch's personal stash.

He purchased new wool clothing, boots, a sword and shield, along with a dragon scale vest to hide underneath his clothing just in case. The thought of heading back to the ship crossed his mind when he was done. Until a certain aroma filled the air that caused his stomach to growl in delight. That smell of baked goods and cooking meats with mead to drink had now taken its place in his mind.

Leon followed the smell until he happened upon an old tavern called Ironside. Inside the place was filled with beautiful women and drunken soldiers. Probably not a place where knights of the castle would keep their reputations intact. He walked inside taking a seat at the bar, the barkeep asked what he could get him. The young man asked for some stew and a cup of mead.

He was sitting at the bar taking in the sounds of the men yelling at one another while the women giggled as they stole the mens coin pouches. A plate and mug being tossed on the bartop behind him made the young man jump. Leon kindly thanked the overly large sized man and threw a few coins at him to pay for his food.

The food wasn't half bad and the mead was getting the job done as well. While he was eating a young lady took a seat beside him and tried to make small talk. She had shoulder length black hair and big blue eyes that could melt the hearts of most men. But to him it didn't seem like a place like her would want to be seen at, nor work for that matter.

"So what brings you to a place like this?" She asked him.

"If you're trying to steal my coin pouch it isn't going to work,"

Leon responded. "I've been watching how you ladies distract these men here while another sneaks up and takes the money."

She laughed at his boldness, "You think that I am one of these tavern whores?"

"Not at first glance, but looks can be deceiving."

"You have me there." She smirked, "Let me reassure you that I am not one of the females that work here."

Leon took the last drink of his mead and wiped his lips, "Then what are you doing in here?" He asked.

"Hiding," she whispered.

"From who?"

She took a quick glance around the bar before ducking her head, "See those two guys that just walked in?"

He took a glance back, it looked like two knights from possibly a neighboring kingdom walked inside the tavern. Leon was hoping that these were not the men she was running from, but something told him otherwise. "What did you do to have knights from the royal guard chasing you around?" He asked.

"Long story."

"Humor me."

"Tell you what. You help me get out of here and I will tell you what you want to know. Deal?"

"Deal," he said. Looking around the tavern a second time gave the impression that getting out unnoticed wasn't going to be an easy task. Leon was quick on his feet and came up with a plan that could work if executed properly. "Do as I say and we may get out of here without being spotted by the knights."

"What do you want me to do?" She asked.

"See that man sitting beside you?"

"What about him?"

"Carefully take his coin pouch and hand it to me," he explained.

Without giving it a second thought she reached over and took the coin pouch from the man's belt. "You mean this?" She held the pouch up in the air with a sly grin on her face.

Leon quickly snatched the item from her hand, "Don't do that," he hissed. "We're trying to get out of here not get ourselves into trouble." He took another quick glance around the room to make sure nobody was watching him. With a slight of hand he placed the coin pouch in the man's pocket standing in front of him. "Tell the man beside you that his coin had been stolen."

"Are you sure about this?"

"Trust me."

She cleared her throat and turned to the man beside her and tapped him on the shoulder. "And I didn't think I was going to get any action tonight." He gave a toothless grin and had breath that made her want to puke.

"You're not getting lucky."

"What in the hell did you bother me for if not for fun?"

"That man over there stole your coin when he passed by."

"I'm no fool girl." He laughed, "Not a soul has ever been able to steal from me." The man grabbed for his pouch that was no longer attached to his belt. "I'll be damned!" He shouted. The man was drunk and stumbled over to the accused. Leon wasn't going to wait for them to have a war of words and pushed the drunken man into the sea of people. The end result was a huge brawl breaking out.

"This is the distraction we needed," Leon said. "Let's get out of here."

Once they were standing far enough away from the tavern both stopped to rest for a moment and catch their breath. Thinking they were safe Leon was about to ask the question on his mind. But that would have to be saved for later as someone walked out of the shadows and into the eerie glow of the street lanterns. It was a man, older looking, long gray and black hair, a full beard and a patch over his right eye.

"Why must you always run away?" He asked, his voice was harsh and raspy which added more to his already grizzly looking demeanor.

"Why must you always keep me under lock and key?" She spate.

The man sighed, "I only wish to keep you safe princess."

"You're a princess?" Leon gasped.

"Don't give me that look." She hissed.

"That she is, boy," the man interrupted. "Her name is Princess Leladda, heir to the throne of Zetaihan. And I am her protector, Brolene. Whatever business you have with her I suggest you walk away and don't look back."

"I will not go back to the castle to be locked up again like some animal!" Leladda belted. "If my father found out about this, he would have you executed."

"Your father is nowhere to be found now is he?" Brolene chuckled.

"That's why I am leaving to find him."

"I'm afraid I can't allow you to do that."

"Try and stop me!"

"Princess, if you refuse to do as you're told I will have no choice but to use other means to subdue you."

Leon drew his blade, "That's not something you say to a person you wish to protect."

"You would draw your blade on a Knight Of Zetaihan?" Brolene's brow furrowed, the light from the lanterns made him look more menacing.

"What are you doing?" Leladda whispered to Leon.

"Protecting you," Leon answered.

"I don't need you to protect me."

"Do you think he's just going to let you go?"

"Brolene will not hurt me."

"But he will kill me and lock you back up until he's done with whatever he has planned," Leon insisted.

"Smart." Brolene laughed, "Perhaps too smart."

"You would kill an innocent?" She gasped.

"He's merely a peasant. Who would miss him?" Brolene unsheathed his blade, "Let's make this quick, boy. I have other business to attend too."

"I demand you both lower your blades!" Leladda shouted.

"I do not take orders from you princess." Brolene shrugged, "Besides, you're just a head that will play a role in the grand scheme of things."

"I will do no such things!"

"Like you will have a choice?" He turned his attention back on Leon, "Time for you to die. It's nothing personal, you were just in the wrong place at the wrong time."

Leon smiled, "If you think it's going to be that easy, make the first move."

"An insignificant child such as yourself is offering me to attack first. Are you mad?"

"Try me." Leon made a motion with his hand waving him on.

"As you wish." Brolene rushed towards the young man with blinding speed. In his mind he was going to strike the young man down with one swift blow. This would all be over soon and when he gets the princess back to the castle he would make for certain she never escaped again. But those thoughts would be short lived. As Leon blocked the blade with his own.

Leon smirked, "You look surprised."

"Unexpected is all," Brolene said.

"Then you'll enjoy this." Leon pushed the man back and swung his sword. Brolene was just quick enough to duck underneath the oncoming attack. He swung his sword upward to counter Leon's attack with one of his own. The young man jumped back and the tip of the blade barely struck his light armor.

"Not bad."

"Likewise."

"Unfortunately it's time to end this fight."

Footsteps and screaming could be heard coming from the darkness. Brolene's men must be on their way was Leon's first thought, and he didn't have the time nor the energy. "Couldn't agree with you more," he said. Holding up his free hand he began to mumble a few words under his breath. A small orb of light appeared in the palm of his hand, "Cover your eyes!" He turned to Leladda and shouted before crushing the orb causing an explosion of blinding light that stunned Brolene.

Leon grabbed her by the hand and pulled her along as he ran. They would run when they could and kept to the shadows keeping out of sight. When they got to the port, he pointed out the ship and talked her into following him onboard.

CHAPTER THREE

GAWAIN'S DELIMA

Gawain paced back and forth, anger beaming from his face when he looked over at Leon. "How could you do this?" He shouted. "This will only make things harder for us. What were you thinking?"

"I just wanted to explore the city," Leon said. "I have been a prisoner on this ship for the past two years. All I wanted was some time to myself, Gawain."

"You're Gawain?" Leladda interrupted.

"I am a young lady. Why do you ask?" Gawain responded.

"Leader of a mercenary group?"

"One and the same," said Gawain. "Again, why are you asking?"

"I am the one that has summoned you here," Leladda replied.

"You?"

"Do you have a problem?"

"No, I just have a hard time believing your story. What is your name?"

"My name is Princess Leladda," she answered. "You are here to do my bidding."

"You're the person of importance I am to escort?" Gawain asked.

"If that is the case, how did you end up here with Leon?"

Leladda told the story of how Brolene had been treating her after her father went on his expedition for an artifact of grave importance. How her mother started to change and always locked herself in her room. Leaving Brolene in charge of running the castle and making decisions in place of the King and Queen. Each time taking one step closer to his true intention of becoming the new King Of Zetaihan.

"Troubling news indeed for you young lady," said Gawain. "What would you have me do?"

"Help me find my father," she said fighting back the tears.

"Where would we start?"

"We should head for Evorian, it was the last news I had gotten from him in a letter he had sent me."

"Let's talk coin," Gawain said.

"Can we not just help her?" Leon interrupted.

"Stay out of this Leon, we need compensation for a job done. It is the only way these men can feed their families."

"As stated in the letter sent to you. I will pay you two hundred gold coins and four hundred silver coins up front. The rest you shall get when we find my father," Leladda explained.

"And where is this coin you offer?" Gawain asked.

She pulled out a coin bag from under her garment and tossed it over to him. "Here's your first payment, like I said, you get the rest when we find my father," she said.

Gawain turned and tossed the bag to one of his men standing beside him. "You know what to do," he told him. "Tell me Princess, how much do you know about the Kingdom Of Evorian?"

"Not much," she answered.

"Allow me to share some information with you," he said. "The kingdom sits on a small island, out in the middle of the ocean. On top of that it's not an easy task to get there. The storms that you must sail through wreck even the most durable of ships. And if you make it even close to the island a creature beyond your imagination lies in wait."

"Sounds like fun," Leon said.

Gawain wasn't pleased with the remarks from the young man, but Aurelius seemed ready for an adventure as well. "I couldn't agree more. Also if we do make it to Evorian and the legend is true, then there will be plenty of beautiful women waiting."

"Women that will kill and eat us if we do the slightest thing wrong," Gawain retorted.

"A woman after my own heart," Aurelius jokes.

"Literally."

"Looks like you will be in need of my services after all," Bosch said.

"We just need your ship," Gawain smuggly replied.

Bosch slyly smiled, "Do you know where the island is located?"

"Shouldn't be too hard to find."

"Not with my help."

"You know the location?" Aurelius asked.

"That I do."

"And how much will that cost us?"

"You can't be serious!" Leon hissed.

"As much as I hate this traitor and wish to kill him," Gawain started. "Sometimes you have to work with the enemy to reach a common goal."

"The Gawain I remember would rather die than work with scum like this." Leon spate.

"People change," said Gawain. "For better or worse, people change."

"Name your price." Aurelius interrupted.

"Straight to the point as usual." Bosch laughed, "For one, you promise to spare my life. Second, once you're done borrowing my ship we part ways and never see each other again. Deal?"

He held out his hand and Aurelius took hold of his wrist, "You have a deal." Aurelius pulled Bosch in closer, "But know that if you try and betray us, I will end your life myself."

"I don't like this," Leon muttered under his breath.

Again the vessel and its passengers found themselves in rough waters. The waves crashed into the sides of the ship threatening to capsize the colossale vessel. Rain and hail pelted the crew and deck hands, the man in the birdsnest was holding on for dear life. If they wouldn't have taken down the main mass it would have snapped in half.

"Why don't you use that orb of yours to calm the weather?!" Bosch shouted at Aurelius.

"I've tried," Aurelius responded. "It doesn't seem to work here."

"Can't you feel it?" Leon called out.

"Feel what?" Aurelius asked.

"The power that protects these waters."

"Could it be the creature your friend spoke of?" Bosch questioned.

"This is beyond what a mere sea creature can do," Gawain interrupted. "It feels like something or someone with a great knowledge of magic is trying to keep us away from the island!"

"What do we do?"

"We have to allow Boch to command his ship and hope for the best."

"This ship has survived worse," Bosch responded. He started yelling out orders to his crew to drop the sails, get to the oars and start paddling. Bosch jumped over the ship's wheel and spun hard to the right, when the ship was in the right position he grabbed hold of the wheel once again. "Raise the mainsail only! We shall use the wind to our advantage, and at this speed the creature will have no chance to strike at us!"

At the knots the ship was traveling it felt like the vessel was going to shake itself apart before they got to the island. "Land ahead!" The lookout shouted. As the ship quickly approached the island a snake-like creature appeared out of the water before them. At a closer glance it almost in some ways resembled a dragon.

Leon could feel the power radiating off the creature and he could tell this wasn't some mere creature of the sea. If it was a dragon, it was one he had never seen or heard of before. In his mind all dragons had wings and flew through the sky breathing fire. This would be the first he had ever witnessed a water dragon.

"Why does the creature not attack?" Aurelius yelled.

"Does it matter?" Gawain said in return.

Bosch said not a word, he focused on sailing his ship around the creature with haste. That's when he caught a glimpse of the young man standing on the outer hull of the ship. It was as though he was looking into the creature's soul. What made things more interesting the young man and the creature had a faint blue light emanating from them both.

Passing by Leon kept his eyes on the creature as it did the same to him. Like the time before he heard a voice in his head, "Beware of the island chosen one, a power you have yet to face awaits there for you. But there is something on the island you must find that will help you on your quest," the voice said.

Land was vastly approaching if Bosch didn't control his ship with precision he could hit the rocks sinking the vessel. The Captain was well known for a reason and not just for his shady dealings. He was one of the best to steer a ship, most pirates and captains of the armades couldn't match his skill.

The ship swiftly made it to some sort of makeshift port. It didn't connect to a city or village. The port connected to nothing but land and that land lead into a wooded area. Aurelius and Leon were packing their bags with only the provisions that were needed. Gawain and his men were doing the same. While Catherine and the few students she brought were getting ready as well. Jefferey, on the other hand, was ordered to keep an eye on Bosch as he still couldn't be trusted.

Gawain had ordered a few of his men to stay behind and keep an eye on the ship and its crew. While the rest of them made their way towards Evorian. Something about the woods was off, it felt wrong, as if it was under a spell or was filled with evil magic. The trees seemed to be alive, twisting and turning as the group made their way further inside.

"Anybody know where this place is located?" Leon quietly asked.

"That is why you needed me," Bosch said. He took out a horn made out of what looked like a type of bone and blew into it. The sound was loud and dark filling the air with an ominous presence. "Listen to me closely. Whatever happens next do not draw your weapons, they will take offence to it. You have to act a certain way, follow my lead and things should go smoothly."

"And if we don't?" Leon asked.

"Then prepare to be cooked alive."

Not long after the group found themselves surrounded by these strange animalistic creatures. They carried spears and small shields readied if needed. Bosch stepped forward holding his hands up in the air, "It is me, Captain Bosch. I am here to make another delivery to your Queen, these are my newest recruits," he announced.

One of those things walked up to them and removed the mask made out of bone. Underneath was a face of a woman, her eyes piercing her face scared from many battles. It was clear she was the one in charge next to the Queen. "What have you brought us?" She asked.

"Weapons of your choice," Bosch answered.

"Show us," she demanded.

"Not this time."

"Why?!"

"I want an exchange."

"That is not the deal that was made," she hissed.

"By all means keep carrying around those sticks," he laughed.

She held the tip of the spear up to his throat, "It has done well for killing so far," she smiled.

Bosch pushed the spear away from his throat, "All I ask is information from your Queen, then you can have these fine weapons."

"Show me them first."

"If that is what it takes," he said. Bosch snapped his fingers and a couple of his men carrying a wooden crate walked up and set it down on the ground. The two men opened the chest and inside was filled with swords and shields, along with light armor that would fit the women perfectly. "Does this please you?" He asked.

"Indeed."

"Do we have a deal?"

"I will talk with the Queen on your behalf."

Bosch turned and motioned for his men to close the chest, then he had words with Aurelius and the others. "Keep to yourselves and say not a word. Follow those two rules and you will stay alive long enough to leave here with your hide intact."

The group of women lead them through the woods, avoiding traps for trespassers along the way. One of Bosch's men was an unfortunate casualty of those traps. He strayed off the beaten path and Bosch watched him do so without saying a word. When the man walked through the trip cord triggering the trap. Wooden spikes came down out of the trees killing him instantly.

The group came to an area that was blocked off by what looked to be layers of mud and trees. Though that didn't stop the women, they pushed part of the debris aside and walked straight through and the men followed them. It was surprising to see that the kingdom of Evorian was made of nothing more than tents and small huts made out of sticks and trees. And what lit up the city was nothing more than campfires at every corner.

It was guessed that the Queen's hut was the largest one in the center of everything. "Stay here and I shall go talk with the Queen," she said. "Watch them. Make sure they don't try anything, if they move kill them." She commanded the others.

"I assure you we just ask for information," Bosch reassured her before she disappeared inside the hut.

"Do you think Aurelius and Leladda are still out there?" Leon whispered.

Gawain took some reptile looking animal out of his bag and

placed it on the ground. The thing took off running into the woods without being spotted by the guards. In a matter of minutes it came back and ran up his leg, up his shoulder stopping at his ear. Then it went back down and back into the bag Gawain had removed it from. "They are out there watching, making sure to stay out of sight," Gawain answered.

"How do you know that?" Leon questioned.

"That's enough talking." One of the women snapped.

"I apologize for my mens brashness," Bosch said. "They will be dealt with accordingly."

"See that they stay quiet unless spoken too."

"Is there a problem?" The lady in charge asked when walking out of the hut.

"Nothing that we couldn't handle, Alkippe."

"Can we see the Queen now?" Bosch asked.

"Only you are allowed to enter Bosch, your men will stay out here."

"As you wish." Bosch bowed.

"This was not part of the plan," said Gawain.

"Stay your tongue!" Alkippe commanded.

Leon stepped in front of Gawain, "Forgive him, it has been a long journey. Do what you must, Captain Bosch." Calling that man a Captain of anything made his stomach turn. But they had to play along for this to work, there was no other way.

Hearing that was enough to keep Alkippe's temper in check, at least for the time being. She turned and walked Bosch inside the hut to have an audience with the Queen as promised. The audience didn't last long as Bosch was escorted back out about ten minutes later.

"As per our agreement the chest is all yours," Bosch told her.

Alkippe could barely contain her excitement as she spoke, "These will aid us greatly, you have done good this time Bosch." She smiled for the first time.

"I aim to please," he said with a crooked smirk.

"Take your men and go," she said. "You have been granted enough time here. Be grateful we are allowing all of your men to leave unharmed."

"And I thank you for your kindness." Bosch bowed once more. "You heard the lady let's be on our way."

Once out of Evorian, and far enough away to make sure they were not being followed. The groups reunited with one another, and decided to set up camp for just a short while. After the injured had been taken care of and food had been eaten. It wasn't long after that Princess Leladda had questions that she wanted answered.

"Did you find anything out about my father?" Leladda questioned.

"Perhaps," Bosch replied.

"Answer her!" Gawain demanded.

"I don't think so," Bosch smuggly responded.

"Why do you refuse to tell her?" Leon asked.

"Because he wants something in return," Aurelius interrupted.

Gawain removed his knife and held it up against Bosch's throat, "Perhaps I have my vengeance right here and now," he spate.

"Go ahead." Bosch laughed, "Then the knowledge of her father dies with me. Plus I am the only one that can get you off this island, have fun being trapped here with these blood thirsty women."

Gawain lowered the blade, "Haven't we given you enough?"

"You have for now," he answered, turning his attention back to the girl. "But she hasn't."

"What do you want from me?" The Princess asked.

"I have knowledge of your father that you desperately want, right?"

"Yes, more than anything."

"What are you willing to give for this information?"

"Depends on what you want."

"The truth is all I ask for."

"You already know the truth."

"Only a small portion."

"What are you getting at, Bosch?" Aurelius snapped.

"That she knows something that she's not willing to share with the rest of us," Bosch answered. "Now tell me girl, what is your father really after?"

"That is Princess to you!"

"In my world there is no royalty or figure heads such as yourselves."

"That is because you're pirate scum! The laws mean nothing to you!"

Bosch smirked, "Say what you will but we still get rich off of people like you."

"What is that supposed to mean?"

He waved his hand in the air, "This conversation is getting old," he said. "Answer my question and I will tell you about your father."

Leladda stared at the ground whispering words to herself, when Leon reached over and placed his hand on her shoulder. "You can trust us," he smiled. "Him not so much, but worry not, he holds no power here," he added. "If you don't trust in Gawain and his men then he can't help you."

She looked up at him and sighed, "My father is after Hades's eye," she finally answered.

"What is that?" Leon questioned.

"It's nothing more than a fairy tale is what it is," Bosch grunted.

"That's not true!" Leladda screamed at him. "My father believes it exists and is risking everything to find it!"

"A fool's errand if you ask me."

"Will someone explain to me what a Hades's eye is?" Leon questioned.

"It's an artifact of great power that allows you to speak to the dead," Aurelius explained.

"Why would your father be after something like that?"

"He wishes to speak to his wife and my mother," she answered. "It's been so long and he misses her dearly as do I. When he caught wind of Hades's eye actually existing. He formed a crusade out of his best Knights and went on the hunt, I haven't heard from him since."

"Thought you said your Mom was back at the castle?" Leon questioned.

"I lied."

"So who is back at the castle waiting for your return?" Gawain asked.

"Nobody," she replied. "I have been the one trying to run the kingdom, but Brolene over rules me. I have been doing this on my own for months now."

"Is that good enough for you, Bosch?" Aurelius snarled.

"Not in the least," he said. "But a deal is a deal. Your father was here, may still be on this island yet."

"What?" She gasped.

"Calm yourself, I said may still be here. From what I gather he was on this island looking for clues of the whereabouts of Hades's eye. The Queen told him of a graveyard on this island. Where the dead have clues to such things if you can convince them to speak with you. But legend has it if you're not strong enough the graveyard will steal your soul away. That is why they dare not go there."

"What makes you think he may still be here?"

"Because the Queen has the sea watched carefully, and his ship was never spotted leaving from the port."

Leladda jumped to her feet, "If he's in danger we must hurry," she said with urgency.

"I'm afraid it doesn't work that way," Bosch responded. "Only four of us can enter the graveyard. Decide who goes and who stays."

Leladda was quick with her response, "I'm going."

"That is not wise," Gawain said.

"Try and stop me." She stared at him angrily.

"Wouldn't dream of it."

"Who else will be going?" Leon asked.

"Bosch will be going," Gawain answered.

"Lucky me," Bosch replied. "Who else will be joining us?"

"Count me in," Leon said. "Who will be the forth?"

"Me," Gawain said.

"I believe I should be the forth," Aurelius insisted.

"Can't let that happen."

"But you should stay behind with your group."

"I will trust you with that task," Gawain said. "As the one that took the job I must see through to the end."

"I will say no more. Be safe out there."

"Likewise."

Cathrine walked up and gave Gawain a hug and a kiss, "For luck," she smiled.

"I need to go on missions with you more often." He sheepishly smiled.

The trek further into the woods was a tedious one, not only that the atmosphere was starting to change. The air was dense and it was getting harder for them to breath. The trees began to change, they looked warped, dead if you will. Fog was forming from the ground up, and it felt like the temperature was dropping fast. Investigating the trees revealed a map to the location of the graveyard itself at least that's what Bosch had explained.

There were markings with different shapes in different locations, deciphore one marking incorrectly and it could spell doom for them all. But Bosch knew what he had to do and led them down the correct path. He could try and screw them over giving him a chance to escape. But there's no guarantee he would survive whatever shit storm he would let loose.

It was clear they had found themselves in the graveyard, the feeling was ominous and appresing. If they weren't strong enough their life force would be sucked right out of them. The graves were marked by wooden crosses and some had plates of armor and swords placed on them. It was unclear if this was a graveyard or battle sight or perhaps both.

Fireflies of many different colors filled the air, and it looked like shapes were taking form within the fog. Though no spirits had approached them as of yet. That is until Leon called out to them getting the attention of a spirit that formed a shape of a rugged battleworn looking man.

"Who dares enter this place of great resting?"

"We only ask of aid-" Gawain began but was quickly cut off by the spirit.

"I only speak to the one that called out to me!"

"That was me." Leon stepped forward, "We only ask for your aid in our quest."

"Why would we help you?" But the ghostly man took a closer look at Leon. He was different from the others that have trespassed on these hallowed grounds. They were weak minded fools in search of riches, that sold their souls to get what they wanted. He sensed that a great power dwelled within this living being. That has allowed him to communicate with the spirit realm before. The spirit also sensed that the young man carried something of great importance and he wanted it.

"Perhaps we can be of help to each other." Leon suggested.

"Perhaps we can. You carry an amulet on you, hand it over and I shall aid you anyway that I can."

"What would a spirit want with my amulet?"

"That is none of your concern."

"I am afraid that I cannot give you the amulet it will be of great use to me in the future."

"Then I'm afraid you and your friends will stay here with us forever!" The spirited angrily proclaimed.

A voice came to Leon yet again, telling him not to fear the undead. Letting him know to stand strong and unwavering and do not buckle under the power of the spirit. "Do your worst spirit, I am not afraid of you! I will prove my strength and you shall do as I say!" He was confident in his words.

"You will regret those words." The spirit was mumbling words under his breath.

"Is he about to cast a spell?" Gawain muttered. "Only a wrath can cast spells." That's when it dawned upon him of what Leon was dealing with, "Leon! Get away from that spirit, it's not what you think!" The young man glanced over at Gawain and cracked a faint smile. "What in the hell does he think he's doing." He clenched his fist tightly. "He's going to get himself killed."

Leon was firm with his stance and refused to give an inch to the spirit before him. Whatever the spirit had been doing he must have completed it as dark fog surrounded the young man. Growing thicker and thicker until Leon was engulfed in the darkness.

"Leon!" Leladda cried out.

"Don't worry you will all be joining him soon enough." The spirit laughed. She drew her blade readying herself to attack the spirit before her, "Do you really think that blade will do you any good against me?" But what the entity didn't expect was Leon using his sword to cut through the spell he had cast. "Nobody can break that seal speal! Nobody! What are you?"

"Your ending if you don't do as I say," Leon said.

Bosch looked on, realizing the same blue aura surrounded Leon's body once again. As a pirate he has witnessed many spells, and ones from powerful wraths like these are damn near impossible to fight against. But Leon held his own against such power and came out unscathed. "That boy's power is what Alistair must fear," he muttered.

The wrath was seathing and yet a bit of fear filled its eyes. Wanting to cast another spell that would be stronger than the last seemed futile. These trespassers were stronger than all the others. "What is it that you seek?" The wrath asked.

Leon sheathed his blade, "That's better," he said. "Tell me wrath, are you the one that controls the weather close to this island?"

"The island protects itself," the wrath answered. "That has nothing to do with me or the graveyard."

Leon examined the area, "How did this graveyard come to be?" He asked.

"A battle from The Great War took place on this island. But you already knew that seeing how you've been to the other realm."

Leon ignored the last thing the wrath had said and asked another question to counter, "Was there a man here earlier with a group of knights?"

"Come to think of it there was," the wrath replied. "The King was a very persistent man. He made me a deal that I couldn't refuse."

"And what deal was that?!" The Princess shouted.

"Aw, you must be the King's daughter."

"Just answer her question, Wrath!" Leon demanded.

"You sure you want to know about your father's darker side?"

"Stop playing mind games!" She screamed.

"Let's say I got to feast on some of his men's souls for exchange of safe passage off this island and information."

"My father would never do that!"

"But he did," the wrath insisted. "All to find the whereabouts of Hades's Eye."

"And after that?" Leon questioned.

"I sent him to the Tomb Of Carnage. But he will not be granted access."

"Why is that?"

"He does not have the amulet that you possess."

"It wouldn't do any good, the amulet has lost its power."

"The amulet needs something special to help it regain its strength."

"Such as?"

"A soul."

"Thank you for the information." Leon took up his sword and swung down through the air. And with his powers aiding him he was able to destroy the wrath. He took the amulet from around his neck and held it up. Whatever soul or souls had been left from the wrath, was sucked into the stone of the amulet. When Leon turned around all of his companions were giving him the look. "What?" Leon shrugged. "One less wrath in the world to deal with."

CHAPTER FOUR

ULRICH LEARNS THE TRUTH

The Kingdom of Drasal was undergoing a drastic change with Alistair being king for the past couple of years. Most of his Knights were replaced with his new minions called the Dark Knights. Men not of the living nor the dead, cursed to serve the one that controls the Reaper Blade. Only a select few were deemed worthy to stand at Alistair's side. Such men as Sir Caine and young knight in the making, Ulrich.

After the Academy was burned to the ground and the students and teachers were done away with. King Alistair had it rebuilt in his image, but when he felt his young students were ready he would have them transformed into one of the Dark Ones. Anyone that went against the King was either thrown in the dungeons or executed.

King Alistair also waged war on any other kingdom that would oppose his will. With the Dark Knights at his disposal the few that did fight against him quickly learned a tough lesson. Follow the new world order or be disposed of. And it wasn't long before kingdoms fell before him and his hordes of Dark knights.

Ulrich was outside training with the new masters, learning the ways of the dark arts. Something that was never allowed back when Edward became king. Caine approached in his new silver armor that Alistair bestowed upon him.

When Ulrich noticed Caine he kneeled before him, "First Knight Caine, what do I owe this humble visit?"

"Do not kneel," Caine said. "You know I hate when you do that."

Ulrich got to his feet and laughed, "That's why I do it," he said.

"Be serious for once, Ulrich."

"Yes, sir," he sighed. "What do you need from me?"

"It's time you take control of your destiny," Caine said. "Zerius thinks you're ready to seek him out. You know where to find him and I suggest you do so as quickly as possible."

"Why the change of heart?"

"Alistair is losing himself to the power of the blade. If we don't stop him now he will ruin all that we have set in motion."

"But he controls the blade."

"Though we both know who the blade is meant for."

"Even if I'm not strong enough?"

"That is why it is important you start your training with, Zerius."

"I see," Ulrich said. "Should I take anyone with me?"

"This trial is only meant for you."

"Then I shall take my leave at once."

"See that you do, it's not a good idea to keep Zerius waiting for too long."

Ulrich packed his bags made from cowhide with all the essentials needed for a long journey such as his. If he remembered correctly it will take him a few days to get to the Dragon Graveyard. A memory shot through his mind like a bolt of lightning. His heart had wished it hadn't as he felt the pain of Ellyn and once good friend Leon's betrayal. He quickly shrugged it off as feelings such as that would only weaken his resolve.

He threw his bags over the back of his favorite horse Nightshade, the animal was given to him as a gift from Sir Caine. The horse was trained well and if you could handle his speed you would fly like the wind. Ulrich hopped on Nightshades back pulled the reins and shouted, "Go!" and off the horse went. The horses hooves hit the ground with a thunderous thud as it ran with Ulrich holding on tight.

After riding for hours the sun was starting to set, and Nightshade was slowing a bit. Ulrich picked out the perfect place to set up camp for the night. It was out in the open where he could be seen easily, not hidden away like a coward the way the old man would do. He invited the challenge of bandits or some other type of being to attack him. It would test how far he had come as a warrior.

Though nothing happened that night, Ulrich did wake up with a sense of pride. Not a lot of people have camped out in the open and lived to tell the tale. The next night he camped would prove to be more than even he could handle. The spirit of his dead sister came to pay him a visit, to warn him of the path he was walking. Pleading with him to change his course and not pursue the dark power.

When he awoke the sun was just peaking its way over the mountains. These emotions that Caine had warned about came at him at full strength and caught him by surprise. Ulrich had to admit that he was succumbing to what he believed was a weakness. And if he had any chance to quill these feelings he would have to train with Zerius and do so quickly. He knew that the dark power would swallow him up if he wasn't confident in his beliefs.

Ulrich spent another half a day riding before making it to the Dragon Graveyard. Before entering another memory overcame him, this was the place where everything changed. This was where he proved that Leon was different. That his friend had been hiding things from him as if he couldn't be trusted. And that Gawain had been in on it as well, just so he could protect his precious student. All while he was left out in the cold, betrayed by them both.

Anger began to stir inside of him, rage filled his heart as he clenched his fists tightly. A familiar feeling came over him again, something he hadn't felt in a while. A strength that came from his hate and rage, a hidden power that he had yet to harness or understand. "There it is," he muttered. "There's what I've been missing for far too long."

Perhaps anger and rage brings out the darkness. Maybe the darkness is stronger than the old man or anyone at the Academy could understand. This could be the power that will help shape the world in the future. These were the thoughts that were swirling around in his head. But this was something he would have to figure out later as it was time to meet with Zerius.

"You're late!" Zerius shouted when Ulrich walked inside the cave.

Ulrich shrugged, "I'm early as far as I'm concerned," he replied. "See that your men look after my horse, he was a gift from Sir Caine."

"That can be arranged," said Zerius. "Have you come to start your training?"

"Why else would I be here?"

"Smart mouthed kid as usual."

"When can I begin my training?"

"Soon," Zerius answered. "For now I want you to explore the cave, make it feel like home. Because you will be spending quite a bit of time here."

"I would prefer to start my training," Ulrich insisted.

Zerius refused as quickly as the words were spoken. It was no longer a request that Ulrich explore the cave but an order to do so from his new master. Out here Alistair nor Caine was in charge, Zerius was, and Ulrich had better realise that quickly. The mage leader held up his finger, it was bony with a razor sharp fingernail protruding out the end. He gave a crooked smile as the tip of his finger caught fire.

"Listen to me boy," Zerius began. "Do as you're told or you will force my hand."

Ulrich laughed turning his back on the mage, "We both know that you won't hurt me." He turned his head slightly to look back at Zerius, "I'm too important for whatever plans you and Caine have in mind. To put you at ease I will do as you say for the time being."

He walked away leaving Zerius standing there fuming at his insolence.

The young man explored the cave, more so than the last time he paid the place a visit. Torches were on each side to light the way, he remembered the way towards the door that allowed entrance into the graveyard. Though he had no reason to go there, he wasn't the chosen one and he would burst into flames if he dared try to enter.

As Ulrich walked he ran his fingertips down the walls. The cave walls felt rigged yet somewhat smooth. Most cave walls the rocks would cut your fingers wide open. This was new to him but not unexpected, the mages had powers that normal humans couldn't even phantom. If they so choose, the mages could change this place anyway they see fit.

As he walked further he could feel eyes upon him, watching his every move. Though he didn't feel threatened it was most uncomfortable. Ulrich pondered if the other mages hated him being there or if they feared him. The latter would be what he hoped for, to him fear meant respect. He still couldn't understand the point of Zerius's wish for him to explore. This was pointless, he was here to train and wanted to get started.

"You have done well," Zerius said as he stepped out of the shadows.

"I don't understand how this is doing well," Ulrich responded.

"You proved you can take orders, though I could do without the lip."

"This was a test?"

"Perhaps." Zerius shrugged, "Perhaps not."

"Which is it?" Ulrich spate.

"Follow me," Zerius demanded, ignoring his new students' words. Ulrich wasn't happy but did as he was asked, keeping close behind his new master. The mage led him to the furthest point of the cave that he had been in so far. It was so dark that Ulrich's eyes had trouble adjusting to the everlasting darkness.

"Stop here," said Zerius.

"But it's pitch black."

"Learn some patience!" Zerius snapped. He muttered some words that Ulrich recognized as dark magic. The torches on the walls sparked one at a time and the cave lit up. Revealing a room instead of another part of the cave.

"How did we get here?" Ulrich gasped.

"This is part of the cave."

"What is this place?"

"Where I come to push myself in the dark arts uninterrupted."

"Why here?"

"This place was built to sustain the powers of the dark arts that I practice. It will ensure the cave does not crumble on top of us when we start the training process."

Excitement flooded over Ulrich's face, "When can we start?" He asked.

"Calm yourself," Zerius grunted. "If your emotions run high, you will never be able to learn what I will teach you."

"My apologies, human emotions are a weakness."

"You only need one emotion to focus on, letting your rage burn bright and harness its power for your own."

"How would I do that?"

"First take a seat in the circle," Zerius told him.

Ulrich did as asked but not without voicing his displeasure, "You would have me meditate?" He grunted.

"Meditation is the key to what you must learn."

"I don't understand."

"This is what I like to call the circle of learning." Ulrich had a lost expression on his face as Zerius spoke, "In other words if you let your true feelings out while meditating it will show you the path you must take. Then after that the training shall begin."

"Shouldn't you already know this?"

"Silence!" Zerius shouted. "Close your eyes and focus!"

Ulrich closed his eyes and let his mind and body become calm, just like he practiced long ago in what felt like another time and place. He breathed in and out clearing his mind of all thoughts waiting for something to happen. "Am I doing this wrong?" He asked. "This feels like a waste of time."

"You have to let your true feelings out for this to work."

"Meditation is about having a calm state of mind."

"True, but this is different. Think about what makes you angry, bring that anger, that rage to the surface and try to control it," Zerius explained.

He kept his eyes closed and only focused on the words that were being said. Before long memories he had tried to suppress broke through to the surface. Images of his family being killed and his sister giving her life to save him flashed before his very eyes. More memories flooded his mind before he had a chance to react.

That of the old man always trying to hold him back. Not allowing him to use the dark arts. Telling him to show mercy to ones that did not deserve such a thing. Scolding him for saying that the townspeople were nothing more than filthy peasants. Then there was Ellyn, he had feelings of great love for her. And yet she, like everyone else betrayed him, left him with these feelings he hated.

The last memory was that of Leon, his best friend, the only one he ever trusted next to Caine. Out of all things Leon's betrayal hurt him the most. It wasn't enough that he hid the fact he had special blood flowing through his veins. He turned against him in his moment of triumph when he helped restore the legendary blade back to its former glory.

It was those memories that made his anger rise, the rage he was feeling took hold. "That's it! Let your rage burn bright! Now fight to take control of it!" Zerius cheered. Ulrich felt a power deep within him grow and grow until it felt like his whole body was on fire. Though he wasn't sure if he was in control or if the power inside was in control of him instead.

Zerius watched with glee as his new student was starting to let the darkness flow through him. A dark aura surrounded Ulrich's body, the power the young man possessed was strong enough that the mage could feel it as well. This brought a faint smile to the man's face, knowing he found the one he had been searching for, for many years.

The dark aura started to fade and Ulrich opened his eyes, a smile of pure evil spread across his face. "I know what I must do," he said with a darker tone to his voice.

"Then let us begin," Zerius replied.

CHAPTER FIVE

FOLLOW THE TRAIL

"Where would you have me take you next?" Bosch question with a hint of annoyance to his voice.

"Any place of our choosing," Aurelius replied. "Remember that if you want to keep your head traitor."

"Have I not done enough to earn your forgiveness?" Bosch jokes.

Aurelius pulled a knife and threw it at Bosch just missing his head by an inch. The blade stuck in the post behind him, "Does that answer your question?" He snarled.

Bosch turned and removed the knife and approached his old friend, "You will never understand what had to be done." He dropped the knife at Aurelius's feet. "Pick it up and use it if you want, but know my men will only listen to me."

"Enough!" Gawain shouted. "We have a mission to accomplish. Bosch if you want to stay alive, live up to your end. Aurelius, if you wish to fight him or kill him, do so after we are done. Now if you don't mind Captain, tell you shipmates to sail north."

"Why north?" Aurelius asked.

"Leladda believes her father would head in that direction."

"So you are willing to blindly do as she says?" Bosch questioned.

"That is what a mercenary does," Gawain responded. "And I believe she is keeping something from us. Once we arrive at the destination of choice I am going to find out what that something is."

"How will you accomplish that?" Aurelius replied.

"I have my ways. Let me handle that when the time comes, besides it is none of your concern."

"As you wish all mighty, Gawain." Aurelius mockingly bowed.

Gawain fumed at Aurelius's childish behavior that much was clear, "Let me know when we make landfall." He turned and walked out of the captain's quarters.

Leon was standing at the stern of the ship, watching the ripples in the ocean water as the vessel sailed towards its destination. It was calming in a way, how the sun shined down on him and a cool breeze blew across his face. For a brief moment he could let go and forget about the world, forget about his so called destiny and the trouble he found himself in.

"It's calming out here isn't it?" Leladda said as she walked up beside him.

"Yeah it is," Leon responded with a smile.

Leladda stretched her arms high into the air and took in the fresh ocean air, "To bad it can't stay like this," she sighed.

"Like what?"

She looked at him and grinned, "Little slow aren't you?"

"Perhaps." Leon laughed, "But nothing lasts forever."

"Can I ask you something?"

Leon shrugged, "Don't see why not," he replied.

"How did you end up here?"

"What do you mean?"

"For one you fight like a knight, even better than some in the royal guard." She assumed he would have an answer but he stayed quiet, "Two, I watched you use magic that eludes even the best of fighters and skilled magic users. Who are you? You're more than just some mercenary."

Leon looked back out towards the sea, "You're right, I'm not a mercenary. I hail from the kingdom of Drasal, Gawain was once my master trainer at the Academy where I trained to become a Knight Of Valor," he explained.

"What happened? Were you exiled?"

"We were betrayed," Leon coldy answered. "The King was killed by his First Knight Alistair. And he became King and burned down the Academy after accusing the Masters of treason. The rest as you can see is evident."

"What about your parents?" She asked.

His facial expression was grim, "They were killed when I was just a small child," he replied.

"By who?"

"The Dark Knights." The memory was still branded into his head like it just happened yesterday. His mother ran to hide him in a secret compartment on the floor. As the Knight's first rode into town wrecking havoc and killing innocents. She told him to be quiet no matter the noises he heard before shutting him inside. The last he could remember after that was Gawain finding him. "Or at least that was what I was told." He spared her the details of the cursed blood flowing through his veins.

"I'm sorry."

"Don't be," Leon responded. "The past is the past, and right now I need to focus on the present."

Leladda gave a faint smile, but asked no more of Leon's situation. Instead both stood there watching the sunset, it was a calm and tranquil moment. Something they both knew they had to enjoy while it lasted, the road ahead was going to be a long and treacherous one.

The next day came bright and early with Gawain grabbing hold of his arm waking him from his slumber. "We've made landfall," Gawain proclaimed. "Gather your things and meet us on the deck, and be quick about it."

Leon muttered a few words of discontent as he was gathering his belongings. He threw his light armor over his undergarments, put on his boots. And went over to where he kept his sword and shield, after strapping his shield to his back he noticed his new sword was missing. Or replaced by whatever was wrapped up in the cloth laying at his feet.

He wasn't exactly happy that someone had stolen the new sword he had just purchased. But curiosity of what was wrapped up in the cloth began to quil his anger. He would get to the bottom of who had taken his blade later, for this felt more important to him for some odd reason. Leon kneeled, slowly reaching out to grab the item that was hidden.

Leon stood with the item in his hands, now unwrapped he couldn't take his eyes off of it. It was a blade but unlike none he had ever seen before. Clearly the sword was old, perhaps from the forgotten times. The hilt closely resembled a dark bronze color, wrapped around it was some foriegn material that formed the grip. Four quillons, two on each side protrude from the cross guard.

A gym that had lost its color was at the bottom of the hilt, in a way it reminded him of the amulet he now carried with him. The blade itself had a strange darkish almost purple tint to it. On top of that the sword was extremely light. He felt like he was holding a feather instead of a blade made from steel.

"What kind of blade is this?" Leon said, in complete awe of what he was holding. Then it hit him all at once, he recognized the blade from the other world where he trained with Robin. "The goddess statue in the church held a blade exactly like this one," he muttered. "Why is it here? And why was it given to me?"

Either way he didn't have time to contemplate the answers, he sheathed the blade to his side and made his way towards the deck. Aurelius and Bosch recognized the blade right away, it was no surprise to Aurelius as he knew Gawain had the blade in the first place. Bosch on the other hand was curious on how all this was going to play out. Perhaps he would stick around a little longer.

"Now that we are all here. Can someone direct us on the path we are taking?" Leon questioned.

"That would fall to our fearless leader, Sir Gawain." Aurelius bowed mockingly yet again.

Gawain's brow furrowed, "Knock it off," he demanded. "This is not a game or some fairytale. Leladda is depending on me to track down her father and I don't intend on letting her down."

"I'm depending on all of you," Leladda said as she approached.

Gawain bowed, "Princess Leladda, we are ready to depart when you are," he informed her.

She frowned, "Don't do that, I hate when people bow to me," she said. "You're a hired hand not a knight in the guard."

"Understood," said Gawain.

"How long will it take to get to our destination?" She asked.

"On foot at least three days," Gawain answered.

"Can we take the horses?"

"I'm afraid that's not possible."

"Is there a reason?"

"The Kingdom Of Medria is surrounded by swamp lands," he responded. "And there are creatures out there that could spook the horses. You should know this already, Princess."

"I do," she hesitantly replied. "I was testing you to see how well your scouts had informed you of this place."

"The girl must think we are stupid," Bosch said. "It's clear she has no memory of this place."

Leladda put her hands on her hips, "How dare you!" She huffed.

"Prove him wrong," Aurelius interrupted. "Should be easy for you, right?"

She nervously swallowed, and her eyes strayed, thinking of something to say that would calm the situation. She was a child when she was out here last. At that time it wasn't a swampland, but instead it was a beautiful forest full of fantastic animals. Not much was said about what happened to the lands surrounding Medria.

It was believed the King and Queen did something to anger the gods, and the land was cursed. Never to be used to help the kingdom prosper like it once did. When they passed many years later, their son and his wife took the crown. But it never changed, the land was still cursed doomed to stay that way forever.

"Last time I was here, I was but a mere child," she answered. "True I don't remember much from that time."

"Then why have you taken us this way if we need to head for the tomb?" Aurelius asked.

"My father hid an object here, that much I can remember."

"What was it?" Gawain questioned. "If I don't know what to look for, I can't help you."

"It was a key."

"To what?"

"A chest that holds Hade's Eye."

"Wait a second," Bosch huffed. "How did you know that?"

"My father's duty as king was to his kingdom and keeping the key safe."

"Then you already knew where your father was going," Aurelius added.

"Is that true?" Leon asked.

Leladda shook her head, "He didn't know the whereabouts of the item. My father was only the protector of the key, enlisting aid to keep it safe," she explained.

"Tell us girl. If your father was just a lackey, why would he seek out the Wrath like he did?" Bosch questioned.

"Hold your tongue," Gawain hissed. "She is my client and a princess that deserves your respect."

Bosch let out a deep and raspy laugh, "I am Captain of a pirate ship, the only thing we respect is the sea," he said.

"See to your ship then," Gawain responded.

"You trust in me enough to leave me to my own devices?"

"Good point. Leon, go with the good captain here and keep an eye on him."

"I prefer him to stay," Leladda demanded.

Aurelius sighed, "Just don't blame me if he ends up dead."

"You've never been able to beat me in a fair fight," Bosch replied.

"Care to find out?"

"Only if you don't use that blasted magic," Bosch responded while walking on ahead. Aurelius followed along arguing the fact that he didn't need magic to beat him in a fight. At first glance it would seem the two were still friends even after the Captain's betrayal.

"Those two still seem to be chummy," Leon muttered.

"Would you not be the same towards Ulrich even after what he has done to us?" Gawain asked smuggly.

"Ulrich's mind was poisoned!" Leon hissed.

"He chose his path!" Gawain shouted back.

"You don't know what you're talking about!"

"Please stop!" Leladda screamed.

"Sorry, Princess." Gawain frowned, "I let my emotions get the better of me."

"I apologize as well," said Leon.

She glared at both of them, "How can you help me if you're too busy fighting," she said angrily.

Jeffrey walked up to Gawain and said something in a low toned voice then went on his way. He nodded as he passed by Leon, something however was different about his friend. Jeffrey looked older, more mature and a little battleworn.

"I was just informed that everything was a go," Gawain told them. "We should leave now if we wish to make it to Medria before nightfall. I doubt that any of us wants to be stuck out there in the dark."

"Before we go I wish to say something," Leladda said.

"Can this not wait?"

"I'm afraid it cannot."

"Go on."

"Look, I'm sure what that miserable man said raised some questions. Allow me to come clean with you both. My father was the guardian of the key that much is true. Guardians are not trusted with the knowledge of the whereabouts of the artifact. It is to protect from ever wishing to use the Eye for self gain. That is why he went to visit with the Wrath. I just wanted you to know that."

"Be honest with us from here on out, no more lies," Gawain told her.

This time was different than the last, the group was large enough to split into two on the island. Here it was advised by Gawain that it would be wise that only three of them made the track to Medria. Not only were there creatures that seemed to enjoy attacking large groups. But men that worshiped the darkness also plagued the lands. Most would call them bandits but Gawain knew better. They enjoyed killing and eating the flesh of others. Which was believed to give them more strength than the normal person.

As they traveled through the woods, Gawain informed them to stick together. Quicksand was a dangerous part of the land and was undetected by the human eye. And Gawain was no stranger to quicksand he had dealt with it many times in his journeys. There was a way to survive being stuck in it. He knew how but doubted the same could be said about the Princess and Leon.

Things seemed normal enough at first glance, lush green land, green full bodied trees with plenty of fruit hanging from the branches. Which caught the attention of Leladda. If the land was cursed as the stories go. Why would the plants and trees be this plentiful? Without giving it a second thought she reached out to take some of the fruit.

Leon was quick to take hold of her wrist, stopping her inches away from the fruit. "What are you doing?" She hissed. "Let go of me!"

"Don't touch anything on these trees or plants," he warned her. "This forest is alive and something tells me it's not in a friendly way."

She glanced over the wooded area, nothing seemed out of the normal. There wasn't anything that led her to believe the plant life would do anything but provide like normal. While his guard was down she picked the fruit from the tree.

"What have you done?" Leon shouted.

Leladda held up the fruit, "See nothing happened, calm down." She caught a glimpse of the blade that Leon was carrying. The hilt of the blade seemed to be glowing a strange blue. "Why is your blade doing that?" She asked.

Leon unsheathed his sword, he didn't have to look at the blades glow to know they were in trouble. He could feel life moving around him, closing in on them to be exact. The fruit growing from the trees and plants was a trap for its prey. Once the fruit was picked the plants would come to life and rip you to shreds. This was not something he was taught, but instead something he could feel.

"Gawain!" Leon called out. "Prepare yourself!"

He already had his blade in hand prepared for battle, "Who picked the fruit?" He questioned.

"Who do you think?"

"What is wrong with the two of you?" She questioned. Within a blink of an eye something had wrapped itself around her ankles. Pulled her to the ground and in an instant lifted her into the air. She found herself upside down and staring straight down at some plant-like creature. Its red eyes glared up at her. But that didn't scare her as much as when it opened its mouth revealing razor sharp teeth.

Leon had to act quickly or Leladda was about to become plant food. He cast a spell of fire to blind the creature momentarily. Leon had a burst of speed when he dashed at the long vine that had Leladda held captive. With one swing of the blade he cut through the vine and the princess dropped to the ground.

He rushed over to her side and helped her to her feet. She assured him that she was alright just a little shaken up. When the flames vanished the plant like creature let out a god awful hiss. It was hungry and planned on making them its meal whether they liked it or not. Gawain made his way over to them after fighting off some of the smaller plant creatures.

They needed to get the hell out of there to survive. But the biggest plant creature used its vines to keep them from escaping.

Allowing the smaller ones to close in on them. Leon though wasn't going to let them die here. He had a friend to save from the darkness, and yes a princess to protect. And even Gawain didn't deserve a fate like this even if he had become an ass.

Leon felt the power that dwelt within him coming to the surface. The blade in his hand seemed to glow even more. Though something told him the blade itself was feeding off his power, possibly bringing the sword back to its former glory. He didn't feel afraid, nor did he feel darkness coming from this blade like he did the other. Again without warning something clicked inside of him. He was losing control, not as bad as before but still he knew what was coming.

It was almost as if the power within him would take over his body. As if to say, if you can't control the power then it shall control you. The blue flames erupted, surrounding his body. He dashed forward with blinding speed. He lifted his sword above his head and swung it down in a slashing motion. The sharp edge blade cut the plant creature in half with little to no effort.

Gawain watched in awe at the level Leon's power was at. His skill as a warrior had improved greatly as well. What mattered most that he could see, was that Leon had matured in his way of thinking. He thought the situation through and came up with a safe way of saving, Leladda. The only problem that still plagued the young man was his lack of control over the power that dwells deep within.

Leladda looked on in shock, it was thc first time she had ever witnessed anything like that before now. She wasn't quite sure what to make of it. Was it skill and use of an unknown magic? Or was it something more that couldn't be grasped by any form of normal?

"Let's go." Leon's voice was deeper, different, almost chilling in a way.

"Leon is right," Gawain said. "We need to get out of here." He cast a spell of wind that knocked the smaller creatures back enough the two could take off running out of the greenery.

The further the three had gotten away the more the atmosphere around them started to change. The sun beat down on them, plant life was scarce except for the occasional cactus growing from the dry brittle ground. And the hot sand mixed with the wind made their lungs burn with every breath they took.

Vultures swarmed high above their heads, which seemed to be the only other form of life except for themselves. Waiting for them to pass out of heat exhaustion so they can peck the flesh from their bones. Every step that was taken seemed unbearable in the extreme heat. Sweat profusely dripped from their brows as they pushed further ahead.

Gawain wiped the beads of sweat from his forehead, "Damn it's hot out here," he hissed. "Would almost have preferred to be eaten by the plants."

"Strange, first time I think I've ever heard you complain," Leon replied with a hint of sarcasm. "Mercenary life make you soft?"

"Don't start this shit again," Leladda grumbled. "Trust me, I'm not in the mood. Save the fighting for later, press on and shut up."

Three days later the ship was back out at sea, the moon was high in the sky and the stars had a certain sparkle to them. Gawain was standing out on the deck joined by Aurelius. He was curious about what happened at Medria. Not a soul had discussed it since returning from the kingdom. All three of them had been tight lipped about their experience, and he wanted to get to the bottom of it.

Gawain gave a light hearted excuse and refused to talk about it further. Until Aurelius pushed the subject refusing to take that lame story of Gawain's as truth. When the truth did come out of his mouth, Aurelius wished he had never pushed for the truth after all. Finding out the Kingdom Of Medria takes up human sacrifices to please their god was a horrible finding. But finding out Leladda's father was going to allow them to be sacrificed was even more horrifying.

"How did you manage to escape?" Aurelius asked.

"Leon."

"Any bloodshed?"

Gawain sighed, "More than I care to talk about."

"Does he remember anything?"

"Not a thing."

"Just like all the times before."

"Pretty much."

"And the girl?"

"Saddened that her father could do such a thing."

Aurelius clinched his teeth, "Did she see what happened with Leon?"

"The good king wanted his daughter to be spared. So no, she didn't get to witness the aftermath of his powers being released."

"Good," said Aurelius. "The less she knows the better."

Gawain took out his pipe and filled it with tabacco, "She's not stupid," he said. He put the bit of the pipe in his mouth and lit the bowl of tobacco. He repeated this ritual until he released a cloud of smoke from his mouth. "We both know it's only a matter of time until she figures out that Leon isn't normal."

Aurelius blew off Gawain's words, "Is she still going to chase after him?" He questioned.

Gawain let out another puff of smoke, "I believe so," he replied.

"Seems a fool's errand to me."

"She paid me to do a job. Until the princess is satisfied then that job is not completed." He took the pipe and emptied out the tobacco into his bag, and put it back into what he liked to call his smoke bag.

"Where to next?"

"You may not like the answer."

"And why is that?"

"We're heading home," Gawain said. "Your home to be more accurate."

"Back to, Rehakadi?" Aurelius questioned with a slight smile on his face. The thought of heading back after being away for many years was almost nostalgic in a way. But something else crossed his mind, they were wanted men in that area. And if Alistair found out they were back could bring trouble to the Elves. "Is that a good idea?"

"It's not," Gawain answered. "But we don't have a choice."

"We need something from the village don't we?"

Gawain yawned and rubbed his eyes, "I'm tired, see you in the morning," he said as he walked away.

"What are you after?!" Aurelius shouted. "Gawain! Gawain! I need an answer!"

CHAPTER SIX

FINDING A BROTHER

Five people in suits of armor on horseback attempted to cross the roughest terrain imaginable. It was once a valley full of lush greenery, wildlife that could feed humans for a lifetime roamed these lands. And crops a plenty feed farmers and townspeople alike. Though that seemed like a lifetime to these riders.

One of them was on the battlefield when everything changed that day. When King Aidan had his men fired a cannon of great destructive power aimed at his enemies. The blast obliterated everything within a thirty mile radius. Charred land, burnt the trees to ash, and turned the knights on the battlefield into nothing more than bodies burned to their armor. Making them look like hideous statues.

If not for the brave souls that she traveled with, she too would be apart of this timeless graveyard. But why come back to such a place? Why relive such horrible memories? Because she was on a mission and the guard was there to support and protect her, whether she liked it or not. Not only did she not like it, she detested it. She was not a kid nor did she feel like being treated as such.

Captain Shena of the Elite Guard led the way making sure Ellyn stayed back and out of harm's way. Troubling times call for drastic measures. And if the bandits or thugs that scoured these lands caught wind of a would be Queen out here in these parts. They would have more trouble than they bargained for.

She smiled at the thought of an ambush, it would be a welcome change of pace. Her knights were well prepared for any and all attacks, and even Ellyn has been well trained to fight. Perhaps she was even better with a blade than herself. Maybe they would find out sooner than later if her thoughts were true.

Movement off in the distance caught her attention. It was moving too fast to be on foot. A scout for the bandits on horseback was the most likely outcome. Could the news of their arrival in these lands have already traveled this fast? Either way she had to prepare them for a possible ambush up ahead.

Shena held up her hand and made a fist, "We will stop here for the moment!" She announced.

Ellyn rode up beside her, "You spotted it too didn't you?" She asked.

"What did you see?"

"A man on horseback."

"How do you know it was a man?"

"I spotted him following us a ways back."

"And you did not think this was important to tell me?" Shena spate

"Thought for sure you already noticed him."

"You have a keen eye, I will give you that," Shena said. "Best be prepared for the bandit scum ahead."

"If you think bandits lay in wait you are sadly mistaken, Shena."

"Who else could it be?"

"I'm sure bandits do not bear signias on their horses," Ellyn replied.

Shena squinted her eyes, it was always a sign that she was deep in thought. "Which kingdom would wish to pursue us? We have treaties that give us permission to be here without incident." Only one would be brazen enough to have them trailed. "King Aidan is the only fool that would pick a fight with us other than the bandits."

"It's not Aidan's men."

"What makes you so sure?"

"Aidan's men have a red signia, this one was brown and oddly shaped," Ellyn told her.

"No worries." Shena smiled and put her helmet back on her head, "I know who it is and they pose no threat to us."

"Do tell."

"Only if you put your helmet on," replied Shena.

"I hate wearing that thing," she snarled.

"Suit yourself. Move on out but proceed with caution just to be safe." She kicked the horse with the heels of her boots letting it know to move onward.

Ellyn did the same all while asking more questions, "Thought you said it was safe. If that's the case why did you tell everyone to proceed with caution?"

"People get desperate in these dark times, remember that." Was the piece of advice that Shena offered. "Now fall back into position princess we shall handle it from here," she commanded.

Ellyn grumbled a few curse words under her breath but did as she was told. As they rode further ahead it was only a matter of time before the scout came back with four others. The armor they wore was old and worn from ages past. The signia wasn't carved into the breast plate like most armor. Instead it was designed as part of the cloth they wore over the front of the armor.

It was clear the one leading the group was in charge of whatever mission they were on. Shena knew who they were and where they hailed from. These knights were from Welux, this place was centered in the middle of a large wooded area. It wasn't much of a kingdom but the people that lived there were prideful either way.

They had a King and Queen along with a very skillful set of knights to protect them all. Crops or clothing, nor making weapons were their strong points. These people earned their coin by the lumber they timbered. Venturing forth after relics were also not something high up on their list. Neither was keeping tabs on a group from another kingdom.

This was out of character for them, which made Shena ponder if something had happened and they were in need of aid. Or if these knights had a more dubious plan of action. Shena removed her helmet as a sign of respect. "To what do we owe this visit?" She asked.

The one in front removed his helmet. He had shoulder length red hair, a twelve o'clock shadow grew on his chin and upper lip. His dark green eyes pierced her blue eyes causing a shiver to run down her spin. "Travel in these parts are prohibited," he announced.

"Since when?" Shena asked.

"For over a week now."

"Is there a reason?"

"There's a dangerous creature roaming these lands. It has halted travel, not even our goods caravan can get through. All that has tried has met an unfortunate end."

"Have you set warriors out to deal with such a thing?"

"The best warriors in the kingdom," he answered.

"Any reports?"

"Unfortunately not."

Shena frowned, "That does not bold well."

"We believe the warriors are dead. That is why we can not allow traveling at this time. You can turn back or we can escort you to our kingdom. Choice is yours."

"I do apologize but we have a mission to accomplish. Turning back now would be futile. If you like we can dispatch the creature that has been terrorizing your people. Going forward for us is the only option."

"You would disobey the laws of this land?" He grunted.

"I see no other choice," Shena responded.

"Then I shall place you under arrest."

Shena laughed, "You can try."

"Do you think I am joking?" The man snarled.

Shena raised a brow, "Is that any way to treat a group of ladies? You tell us to go back and when we refuse you threaten us. On top of that you haven't even introduced yourself. Not very gentlemanly of you now is it?"

The man nodded his head, "Forgive me, I was rather brash. My name is Lance. I hail from the kingdom of Welux," he said. "I humbly request that you turn back before it's too late. I couldn't forgive myself if a beautiful lady such as yourself was eaten by some ugly creature."

Shena could feel her cheeks flush, she turned her head and coughed to hide the fact she was blushing. "Look, Sir Lance-"

"Just Lance," he interrupted.

"Okay, Lance. Like I said before, we refuse to turn back. And we have not the time to visit your kingdom."

Lance sighed, "It would seem we are at an impasse."

"Not really. You can either move or travel with us a way. How did you say it before? The choice is yours."

"And you think you can go at it alone?"

"They do not call us the Elite Guard for nothing," Shena bragged.

"You're telling me the Elite Guard is nothing more than a bunch of women?" His words were harsh and snarky as if to say a woman couldn't be as good of a warrior as a man.

Shena scowled at Lance before putting her helmet back over her head. She spurred her horse on and rode past him without saying another word. Her anger was boiling over, she was tired of proving her worth as a knight. The Elite Guard was nothing but the best women fighters, the former King and Queen saw to that.

Ellyn rode beside Shena trying to get the Captain Of The Elite

Guards attention. Though the attempt was futile, Shena was no longer in a talkative mood. Not only that, she had ushered her horse past Lance and his men. And she refused to turn back even when she warned her to do so. If that wouldn't get them arrested for treason against the crown nothing would.

It was clear that Lance however wasn't one to give up. He followed behind them, staying back enough to keep watch for the creature. Ellyn believed that Shena was on the hunt. The creature would be a welcome challenge instead of being followed by a bunch of pompous jerks. Ellyn wanted to test her metal as well. She had been training hard to improve the skills that were at her disposal.

Lance watched from afar, he kept an eye out for what he felt was hunting them, not the other way around. He tried to warn the lady knights but the one that led the group was too arrogant to hear him out. What they don't know was the beast had been born from the shadows. Only the light from the sun makes the creatures' true appearance visible.

Back in the days of old the beast's name was that of legends. Graveteeth, was the name that sent chills down the spin of man. Lance knew this but others did not. This was not something that was known but something learned. If they would have had this information sooner, those warriors would never have been sent to their deaths.

That is why it was so important for them to be out and police the lands. To make sure all travellers were safe from harm's way, it was the oath of knighthood. Protect the weak, see the lands are safe, and above all else protect the kingdom of, Welux. Now he must protect the women from another kingdom be female knights or not.

Allowing them to face Graveteeth alone was not an option either. They would need the help, and if he were to die, he would do so upholding his knights oath. Lance's hair stood up on the back of his neck. It was in that instance that he realized they were being followed or better yet hunted. The bigger question was when would Graveteeth attack?

Women screaming and men shouting could be heard off to the far left. Lance pulled on the reigns of his horse and spurred it off in that direction and his men followed his lead. Shena was informed by the other riders that something was going on behind them. Shena stopped her horse and turned to see that Lance and his men were riding off in another direction and fast.

Shena wasn't a heartless woman and did not wish ill will towards anyone, not even a pompous ass like Lance. She sighed and motioned for the others to follow in pursuit. Ellyn could hear the commotion coming from just up ahead. The young lady dismounted from the horse and ran ahead on foot. Shena spotted her running ahead but it was too late to try and stop her.

Ellyn acted quickly, perhaps she could see what others could not. She could see some sort of shape forming in the shadows from the sunlight. It was attacking the caravan, unfortunately a few of the travelers had already been killed. There was also a woman trying her best to protect a young child from danger. Ellyn rolled on the ground over in front of them with her blade drawn.

Shena ran up to Ellyn, "What do you think you are doing?"

"Get these two out of here!" Ellyn shouted. "Hurry!"

Shena turned to the woman and child, "Run!" she shouted at them. Shena let the other knights get the woman and child to safety while she stayed behind to aid in the fight.

"Be ready the beast is taking form," Ellyn warned.

"I don't see anything," Shena responded.

"It's there, trust me."

Shadows on the ground started to take shape, forming into a dark mass that floated into the air before them. Lance came running over to give them aid but stopped dead in his tracks. He fought back the fear that swelled in the pit of his stomach. Most that have witnessed the true form of Graveteeth never live to tell the tale.

And yet here he stood watching the inevitable tale of his death play out. He cracked a smile and let a faint laugh slip from his lips. If this was his last day to live he was going to make it a glorious one. He drew his blade and stood ready. When the transformation was over, Graveteeth stood before them in all his glory.

This creature was unlike anything they had ever witnessed. It had the head of a Lion and the body of a griffin. Its claws were razor sharp, one swipe from those things would spell your doom. And if that didn't kill you the venom from the scorpion tail would do the trick. Graveteeth let out a ferocious growl as it prepared to attack.

"I can't believe my eyes," Shena gasped.

"Wish you would have listened to me now?" Lance asked with a hint of sarcasm.

"What do we do?" Ellyn questioned.

"We fight!" Shena said with pride.

Lance smirked, "I like your style."

The beast charged at them like a raging bull, the three barely managed to roll out of harm's way. Graveteeth swiped one of its enormous paws at Lance, he managed to duck just in the nick of time. He stabbed at the creatures paw to no avail. To that thing it probably felt like he was swinging a toothpick.

"Swords will be of little use in this battle!" Lance shouted. "We need to think outside the box!"

The scorpion like tail hurdled towards Ellyn, she sidestepped the attack and swung her blade down to no effect. "He's right, Shena. My sword didn't even pierce the creature," Ellyn proclaimed.

"I'm open to suggestions!" Shena shouted.

Ellyn let out a loud shriek, she had been knocked to the ground and pinned down by the creature. Shena fought to get to the princess, but not even she had the strength to fight such a powerful foe. The combined efforts of Lance and Shena still wasn't enough to help Ellyn. The tail of Graveteeth was poised and ready to strike. Ellyn closed her eyes preparing herself for the end of her journey.

Saddened by the thought that she would never see her brother or sister again. She took a deep breath and awaited her fate, though death did not come. Ellyn opened her eyes in time to watch the great shadow beast being pulled into some type of vortex. The beast howled and clawed at the ground fighting with everything it had not to be pulled in.

But the vortex was stronger and before long Graveteeth was gone and so was the vortex it was sucked into. Shena was quick to Ellyn's side, helping her to her feet. "Are you injured my lady?" Shena questioned.

"I'm not hurt," Ellyn answered. "Are you alright?"

"Do not worry about me."

"Where did the creature go?"

"Sent back to shadows from where it came," Lance responded as he walked up.

"Was that your doing?" Ellyn asked.

"Such magic is beyond my ability," he replied.

"Then who?" Shena questioned.

Ellyn caught a glimpse of a Knight wearing black armor, sitting atop a black steed. A red cape stretched from the shoulders and down the back of the armor itself. Along with a long red feather like material coming from the comb of the helmet. She pointed at the Knight, "Perhaps he had something to do with it," she said.

Shena and Lance looked over in that direction, both drew their blades acting as though they were ready for battle once again. "One of the Dark Knights," Shena gasped. "Could this day get any worse?"

Lance laughed, "Another challenge to face already."

Ellyn shook her head, "He's not a Dark Knight," she told them.

"He looks like one to me," Lance grunted.

"If he were one, he would have attacked," Ellyn replied. "Perhaps he's the one that summoned the vortex to banish, Graveteeth." But something seemed all too familiar about the Knight. She couldn't put her finger on it, she just knew.

"Let's hope he keeps to himself," Shena responded. "We wouldn't stand a chance against someone that strong."

"No need to worry he's already gone," Ellyn told her. She stood there pondering what she was feeling. A sadness rushed over her like one big tidal wave. The feelings she had for Ulrich, and leaving him behind was part of that sadness.

Shena placed a hand on her shoulder, "Are you alright?" She asked, concerned with how the princess was acting.

Ellyn shrugged her hand off, "I'm fine. We need only to focus on finding my brother," she insisted.

CHAPTER SEVEN

PLANTING THE SEEDS

Caine walked inside the King's chamber and kneeled, "My Lord I have news," he announced.

King Alistair stood from his throne, "Lord Caine, please stand. My First Knight needs not kneel to anyone."

Caine stood but still humbly bowed, "You are my King, and I shall have nothing but respect for the man that wears the crown."

Alistair shook his head, "You will never change my friend." He smiled for just a moment, "I believe you said you had news for me?"

"There has been news of an uprising in the west."

"When is there not? I did warn that some would not accept the new world we are trying to create."

"We must stop this before it gets out of control."

Alistair grinned, "You worry too much," he said. "But if it eases your mind then do what you feel you must."

"By what means?"

"Use your own judgement."

"What of the Dark Knights?"

"Do you need their aid?"

Caine thought about it for a moment, "I think I can handle this one on my own."

"Take a few men with you, just to be on the safe side."

"As you wish." Caine bowed and turned to take his leave.

"Oh and one more thing."

Caine looked back slightly, "Yes?"

"How is the hunt for Gawain and the others?"

"Fruitless."

"I see. You may take your leave."

Caine walked into the horses stable and picked out one of his favorite steeds. He threw his saddle and bags over the horses back and jumped on. It was going to be at least a two day ride and he had to be well prepared. And from the rations he gathered he had a good four or five days worth of food and water.

As he rode out of town the people gathered and cheered him, along with a few jeers. Not everyone is going to love him as a knight, but the ones that did would prove useful in the end. The weak minded fools that were easily controlled would do anything to please the new King. The thought made him laugh a little on the inside.

He made his way out of the kingdom and further into the wild terrain. Caine took a deep breath, letting it soak in. It had been a long time since he had last left the castle. Since he had last breathed in fresh air that wasn't polluted by the people he called filth. But even filth can serve a purpose, even an arrogant King as well.

None of that mattered at the moment, it wasn't time to put his plan into motion just yet. He had to focus on the here and now, and letting a rebellion start would work in his favor. As it would distract Alistair for the time being. Though something had to be done if it was going to grab the attention of the King. Caine himself was going to have to ruffle some feathers and he had the perfect plan to accomplish just that.

Caine knew where the rebellion hideout was located, a small farming town towards the west. If his memory served him well, the name of the town was Brixle. And almost all great rebellions started in some small town or another. As he rode into the small dusty town, not a single person gave him the slightest of notice.

He wasn't dressed in the usual knights armor, instead he looked like one of the town beggars or a thief. In his mind that was a good thing, he couldn't very well let his true identity be discovered. If they knew he was Alistair's right hand man he would be killed on the spot. Still though he had to figure out a way to earn their trust. And he had the perfect ruse to make that happen.

He had chosen a couple of his most loyal knights to pull this off. To give their lives for the greater good of the kingdom. The plan was simple, once he was in town. His own men would attack him and the rest would fall into place. Caine rode into town and looked over his surroundings, he noticed two men walking the rooftop of a certain building. That must have been the hideout.

"End of the road for you scum!" A voice shouted.

Caine smilled, in his mind this was going to work out perfectly, "Perhaps! But I won't go down without a fight!" He jumped off his horse and quickly unsheathed his blade.

"Wouldn't have it any other way." One of the knights stayed on his horse and commanded the others to take him down. "Kill him if he doesn't want to go along quietly."

Caine glanced over at the men standing on the roof. Two more men and a woman had joined them, watching the commotion. "Come on then, let's see what you got." He wasn't going to be able to show his true skills with the blade or they might get suspicious. But still he had to make it look convincing.

One of them lunged at him, Caine acted as though he was surprised. Still he showed just a small amount of what he can do with a blade. Allowing the other knight to purposely kick him to the ground. He kicked Caine's sword away and held the tip of the blade to his throat. "What should we do with him now?" He turned to the fake commander and asked.

"Kill him if he doesn't tell us what we want to know."

"You would kill me either way," Caine spat.

An arrow zipped through the air and hit the knight that was holding the blade to Caine's throat in the shoulder. That gave him the opportunity to take out his knife and stab him in the stomach. The young man's eyes widened, he couldn't believe that his comrade in arms had stabbed him. This was supposed to be a ruse, no one was to be hurt and now he found himself bleeding out.

Caine rolled over to his sword and picked it up, jabbing the blade through the others chest. He gave the same look of disbelief as the young man before. Blood gurgled from his mouth as he tried to speak, but Caine quickly stabbed him in the throat before he got the chance. The fake commander tried to get away but was struck down by arrows that hit its mark. He fell from the horse and his lifeless body hit the ground with a thud.

Caine fell to one knee and pretended to be exhausted from what just transpired. A couple of men wearing hoods and black cloaks came up and lifted him to his feet. Rushing him off the street and into what he believed was their hideout. He gave a faint smile, his plan worked to perfection, not even his own men saw it coming until it was too late.

"Get this man something to drink!" One of the cloaked men demanded upon entering the building. Caine figured this man must have been the leader. A lady with long greyish black hair came up with a skin filled with liquid. The man took it and walked to Caine, "Here drink this."

Caine took the skin, "Thank you for your kindness." He took a good long drink before wiping his mouth and handing the skin back over.

"Don't thank me yet stranger," the man said. "Tell me, why were those knights chasing you?"

Caine stood, "My business is my own. And may I please have my sword back?"

The man pondered on it for a second, "Can't allow you to have your weapon back until we know we can trust you," he said.

"What of my horse?"

"Well taken care of."

"And you say you can't trust me?"

"Correct."

"How can I trust you?"

"We did save your life," the man answered.

"I'll give you that." Caine shrugged, "Though you do hide your faces. Does that win trust in others?"

The man removed his hood, showing his facial features, he was older than Caine by at least five or six years. He had brown eyes that burned with pride and hatred. Shoulder length black hair and a little patch of hair on his chin. "Does seeing my face calm your notions?" He asked.

"For the time being."

The man folded his arms and rested them on his chest, "Will you tell me why those knights were after you?" He questioned.

"Not yet."

"Why not?"

"A man with no name cannot be trusted."

The man laughed or growled, it was hard to tell which. "Name is, Stilfadr Bhittagh," he replied.

"Sounds like a barbarian's name," Caine said.

"Is it? Never knew."

"None the less my name is Shawn."

"Not much for jokes are you?"

"Can't say that I am."

Stilfadr studied the man before him, he didn't know if he was exactly trustworthy. Even though he put on a front, something told him the man was more dangerous than he appeared. At first he didn't seem like much while those knights made him look like a fool. But when he fought back that told a different story. The look in his eyes said he would kill you at the drop of a coin.

Caine could sense the barbarian watching him closely. Trying to figure out what his game was. He had to distract the man before he started thinking poorly of him. "Still trying to figure out why those knights were chasing me?"

"Just by looking at you I can tell you're stronger than you act," Stilfadr blurted out.

He had to choose his next words wisely, this barbarian was smarter than the ones he had met in the past. "One should never reveal his hand until it is needed."

Stilfadr was getting irritate that his questions were not being answered honestly. Instead the man before him was intent on playing a game of cat and mouse. Everyone in his group had secrets, but not important enough for King Alistair's knights to give chase. "I have not the time for this nonsense," he grunted. "You may leave this place stranger, but know that loose tongues can get a man killed."

Caine stood from his chair, "You would send me out unarmed?" He smirked. Stilfadr barked out a command and Caine's weapons were brought to him. Caine shuffled through his inventory to make sure all was returned. "Allow me to tell you this. Alistair is planning something, and if he succeeds it will wipe out any and all resistance."

"Why tell me this?"

"I know a resistance when I see one. You saved my life, now I'm trying to save yours."

"Thanks but you're wrong. There is no resistance here we save who we can that is all."

Caine laughed, "Have it your way." He turned and walked out of the building. A smile stretched across his face, he had planted the seeds in the leaders mind. It wouldn't be long before the barbarian acted upon the news he had just received. And Caine was more than happy to come back in a few months time to fuel the fire.

CHAPTER EIGHT

SHADES OF THE OLD GAWAIN RETURN

THE SHIP WAS STILL OUT IN THE OCEAN, THE WIND WAS CALM and not a cloud in the sky. The blue ocean water did not ripple nor did it seem to move the pirate ship in either direction. If the wind didn't pick up the sails were useless. On top of that there weren't enough men to man the oars after the battles from the journey so far.

Something had to be done, Aurelius's magic orb was no longer an option. Somewhere in between the last mission and where they were heading the orb ran out of juice. It was strange, the orb had never lost its power in as many ages the elf village had pertained to it. Perhaps it had to do with the power that dwelled in Leon that drained the orb. There was no way of knowing for sure.

What could be done with a pirate ship that doesn't move? This was the first time that Captain Bosch had ever encountered such a situation. He had heard of such tales on the high seas but never encountered it until now. None had any ideas on how to get the massive vessel moving again, and most die at sea when things like this happen.

"Any ideas on how to get this ship moving again?" Gawain asked.

"Not a clue." Bosch laughed, "You Aurelius?"

He shook his head, "Can't say that I do."

"Are we just supposed to sit here and die?" Leladda exclaimed.

Leon sighed, "I may have an idea," he responded.

"If it will get us moving I'm open to any ideas," said Bosch.

The young man pondered if it would even work, also trying to decide if letting the other two know his secret would be wise. Though there wasn't much of a choice unless he wanted them all to starve to death at sea. "I want to try something, though I'm not sure it will work," Leon explained.

"What are you thinking, Leon?" Gawain questioned. "Don't do anything foolish." The look in his eyes told a familiar story that he had grown accustomed too. Which meant the young man was going to show his hand to the others.

"Don't act like you care," Leon hissed.

"There are certain things you should not unveil about yourself," Gawain warned. "Caring is not the point, being smart is."

"What if I can get the ship moving? Do you have any better ideas?"

"He's right," Aurelius replied. "Unless you can think of something, we are sitting ducks out here."

"You think Bosch needs to know about, Leon?"

"He already knows?"

"How?" Gawain gasped.

"Not sure. But he knows more than he should."

Gawain sighed, "Do what you must, Leon."

"What can he even do?" Leladda asked.

"Quiet girl," Bosch grunted. "Watch and find out for yourself."

Leladda voiced her displeasure with how the Captain had spoken to her. But her attention would soon turn to Leon after he insisted for everyone on deck to be quiet. He closed his eyes and focused, it was his understanding that if he tried maybe he could ask the sea dragon for aid. That is if he could connect with the dragon using telepathy like he had done years ago.

At first there was nothing, just the sound of birds flying over head. Come on, I can do this, he thought to himself. That's when he tapped into the power within him. Leon wasn't sure how he managed it, but it didn't matter. He knew he had limited use over it for the time being and must act wisely. Voices were coming to him, first one at a time along with shapes he could not make out. He was unsure if it was the dead reaching out to him, or creatures from another time long past.

All of a sudden what had been one or two voices at a time became many. It was like a tidal wave that flooded over him all at once, though he had to fight past it. He forced himself to wade through the masses of voices and shadows. Until his mind's eye found what it was looking for, the water dragon.

"Who has invaded my mind?" The dragon rumbled.

"The one you consider the chosen," Leon replied.

"Why have you summoned me?" The fierce bellowing was almost enough to force Leon out of the creatures mind.

"I am in need of your help."

"Then speak!"

"A vessel I travel on is stuck out in the middle of the vast ocean. There is no wind for the sails and the waves stand still as if the gods do not wish for us to keep on our journey," Leon explained.

"It is not the gods that go against you, but the powers of the Dark Ones that try and hinder your goals."

"Will you help me?"

"I am to aid the chosen in his quest or so I am told. Connecting with your mind will show me your location. It is not for me to refuse until my oath is complete."

"Thank you for your aid."

"Do not thank me until the task is done."

Leon opened his eyes, he noticed that everyone on deck was watching him. He gave a faint smile, "Help is on its way," he said before walking off towards the side of the boat.

"Wait up!" Leladda shouted. "What did you mean by help is on the way?"

Leon shrugged, "I asked for help."

"We're out in the middle of the ocean, there's no asking for help. Even if you could, it's not like you can move a vessel such as this," she responded back.

"Do not concern yourself with that, the ship will move soon enough."

Leladda went to respond until the loud thud from underneath the ship caught her attention. She was startled and fear welled up in the pit of her stomach. The thought of a sea creature sinking the ship before she had a chance to confront her father made her extremely angry. Surprisingly, the ship started to move.

She looked up at the sails and they were still down, when she looked over the side of the boat there were no waves that moved them. When Leladda glanced over at Leon he was smiling. Was this the help he had spoken of? She thought to herself. The orb that the elf carried no longer worked. It would take a large amount of magic to move the vessel and she doubted Leon possessed such power.

"By the gods the boy has done it," said Bosch.

"Yet somehow you knew he would," Gawain responded.

"Was it that obvious?"

"You've been keeping a close eye on him, that in itself is obvious," Gawain answered. "Though I believe you know more than you let on."

Bosch shrugged, "At least we're moving." He turned and casually walked away.

"Someone want to explain to me how we're moving?" Leladda asked.

"Aurelius can answer this one." Gawain cracked a faint smile as he walked away as well.

Leladda looked over at Aurelius, "Well?"

Aurelius wasn't sure how much he should reveal about the situation at hand. Knowledge is power and at times that power can be a very dangerous weapon. The young girl is a princess and that will pose a problem if she knows too much. Tell her to little and she will suspect they are hiding something.

"It's okay Aurelius, I will explain things to her," said Leon.

"Is that wise?"

"Is it wise to hide the truth?"

"Think of what she may do with such information."

"And what would I do?" Leladda barked.

"We don't know you, therefore how can we trust you won't use such information against us?"

"As I said Aurelius, I will handle this," Leon interrupted. The tone in his voice was clear that he was getting annoyed. "Give us some privacy."

Aurelius bowed, "As you wish my young friend, just be mindful of the things you are willing to share."

'Now that we're alone. I can answer your question, though you may not believe what I tell you," Leon said.

"Go on, I'm listening," she responded.

"First off, the ship is moving because of me."

Leladda's eyes widened, "How is that possible?"

"A water dragon is underneath moving the vessel to aid us in our quest."

"Dragons have not existed in ages," she said. "You're not being honest with me."

"Dragons still exist," Leon replied. "They have been in hiding since the great war."

Leladda's brow raised, "Even if that were true. How could someone such as yourself contact such an ancient creature?"

Leon's face contorted, as if he was thinking about how to answer the question at hand. "You see." He sighed, "I'm not your normal person, there are things about me you don't know. Hell, I don't even know who or what I am."

Her face had the look of confusion, "What are you trying to say? Are you not human?"

Leon shrugged, "As human as you can get," he said. "Let me try this again." He rubbed the stubble on his chin, "My bloodline is cursed, not sure if I understand it myself. I am considered the chosen one, destined to save or destroy the world. Which means I have certain powers that dwell deep within me. And somehow I can communicate with dragons using my mind."

Her eyes had tears in them as she fought the urge to laugh, though the laughter came anyways. She expected to see a smile on Leon's face or a slight chuckle escaped his lips. But he stood there straight faced, perhaps mad at the fact she didn't believe him.

"You're not joking are you?"

His gaze was piercing, "This is not the time for jokes," he said. "What I have said is the truth."

The look on her face had changed to one of disbelief, nothing he explained made any sense. Cursed blood, powers within and the ability to talk with dragons was outlandish. But the pirate ship was moving without aid from the elements. There had to be some truth to his words even though she chose not to believe him.

"Time to gather the others, we will be making landfall soon," Leon told her.

"Let me guess, the dragon told you this," Leladda sarcastically replied.

Leon smirked, "Perhaps."

Aurelius walked up followed by the others and Lady Cathrine was with them as well. "The good lady here told us, land was near," he said. "Is that true?"

"If she said land was near, then land is near," Gawain grunted

"Calm down, Gawain," Cathrine insisted. "There's no reason to be a hothead."

"Where's Bosch?" Gawain grumbled, ignoring Cathrine's words.

"Right here!" He shouted from the helm of the ship.

"Land ahead!" The man from the birds nest shouted.

"There's your answer," Leon laughed.

Leladda was clearly confused, "How did she know?"

"Young lady, not all is what it seems aboard this ship," Cathrine replied. "I am what one would call a White Mage."

"I thought those with that label only served the church of the goddess?" Leladda asked.

"That's a story for another time," Cathrine said.

"What's everyone else's story?" Leladda asked.

"I'm an Elf that has traveled the world and have been on many adventures, like the one I'm on now," Aurelius said.

"Captain of a pirate ship," Bosch responded. "Think that says it all."

Gawain sighed, "I was once a master trainer at the academy of Drasil," he said.

"How did you end up a mercenary?" Leladda questioned.

Gawain turned his back to the young lady. That was one question he refused to answer. The memory was still fresh in his mind and heart, and speaking of such things did no good. "I was a teacher at the same academy," Cathrine spoke up. "Teacher of magic and healing arts. Until we were betrayed by one of our own. The academy was burnt to the ground, we were the only ones to survive. Gawain, Henry, Jeffrey, Leon and myself."

"Save the rest for another day," Gawain interrupted. "We must prepare for departing."

"Shall I accompany you this time?" Cathrine asked.

"That would be wise," Gawain responded. "You should join us as well, Aurelius."

"What about him?" Aurelius pointed at the Captain.

"Leave him here," Gawain smirked. "He's not going anywhere."

"And how would you know that?" Bosch asked.

"Wouldn't be much of a captain without a ship," Gawain replied.

"What shall I be doing?" Leladda asked.

"You will be coming with us," Leon answered before anyone else could.

"She will be staying behind," Gawain demanded.

"I will most certainly not!" Leladda stomped.

"There's nothing you can do here," Gawain responded.

"She must go!" Leon shouted.

"Why must she go?" Gawain argued.

"The Dragon said we must all go," Leon explained. "Even the captain."

"Then the Dragon better explain why!" Gawain grunted.

Those words must have infuriated the mighty creature, as the ocean water rushed over the sides of the vessel. And the enormous figure came up and out of the water. Just the sheer sight of the dragon made everyone except Leon tremble with fear. It let out a deafening roar that shook the vessel and all aboard.

"She says that one such as herself doesn't need to explain herself to humans," said Leon. "We must repay our debt to her and that request has been made."

"I don't like it," Gawain spat. "If we get caught she will be punished just for being with us."

"Doesn't matter if you like it or not," Leon replied. "This is not our choice to make."

"Then it will be your job to protect her."

"I don't need protection," Leladda objected.

Leon walked up next to her, "She will be just fine," he said.

"Then it's settled," Aurelius said. "Let's prepare ourselves for what's ahead. Also, Allora just may kill us for not coming back sooner."

Leon nodded and then turned to face the dragon, "Thank you again for your help, though I have a feeling you don't care too much for my kind," he said with his mind.

"Your kind takes what they want with no consideration to others or the world around them. They cause pain and suffering, you would scorch the lands around if it got you what you wanted."

"Not all of us are that way."

"Yet your kind caused the great war and corrupted my kindred spirited family to aid you. And thus most of my kind was almost wiped out because of what your people started."

"That was the past."

"And yet here we are."

"We stand against the one doing wrong trying our best to stop them."

"By using powers that you don't understand, which is what caused the great war in the first place."

"I didn't ask for this cursed blood flowing through my veins."

"Yet you use it."

"It just happens, I can't even control it."

"What will happen when you do learn to control it?" Leon hesitated, not sure how to answer the question. "Exactly."

"Then why do you help me?"

"Dragon's keep their promises."

"To who?"

"You will find out soon enough."

"Tell me!"

"It's time for me to take my leave, until we meet again." The dragon let out another mighty roar before diving back down, disappearing back into the ocean.

Leladda stood there in awe, gazing at the magnificent beast before her very eyes. It was a sight to behold, never in a million years would she ever thought she would see a dragon. And a live one at that, it was believed dragons were extinct. Wiped out because of the great war and what transpired afterwards. At first glance it looked like the beast and Leon were staring each other down before diving back down below. It was then she realized the young man had been telling the truth all along.

"What did the dragon have to say?" Cathrine asked.

Leon frowned, "Nothing good."

"Not a surprise," Aurelius said. "Took a while for the Elves to even trust in man again after the great war."

"Though not all of us are bad, just like not all Elves are good," Gawain commented.

"There is good and evil in all of us," said Cathrine. "It is up to us to decide which path we will follow."

"Spoken like a true follower of the light," Bosch laughed.

"Better to be a follower of the light instead of a dirty dog at sea," Cathrine hissed.

"Choose your next words wisely," Gawain warned Bosch. "You are so close to having your freedom back. It would be a shame for something to happen now."

"Whatever you say boss."

"Enough!" Leon shouted. "We have a mission to accomplish here. Or did you forget that?" He turned and stormed off, it seemed as though what the dragon said had him upset.

Again before they departed, this time however they grabbed only what they could carry. The group would have to rely on the land to provide them with food and water. Being weighed down with rations would only slow them down. Leon warned them of the dangers he could sense and moving fast would be a must.

The group was quick to stay within the shadows. Being back on these lands was dangerous indeed. Though Gawain insisted that he must retrieve an item from the elvish town of Rehakadi. And if all possible restore power to Aurelius's orb. If Alistair or Caine caught wind their return it would bring the Dark Ones down upon them.

Allora welcomed them back with open arms happy to see them well. However she wasn't thrilled to see Bosch standing with them. She never cared much for the man that Aurelius called friend. Allora hated the man even more once she heard the story of how things transpired after leaving Rehakadi. She went as far as giving the command that Bosch be locked up for his crimes.

It took some convincing from the others that the Captain be spared for now. She reluctantly agreed after she learned that the water dragon insisted it to be so. Gawain had wished to speak with Allora alone, he claimed it be matters that only concerned him and Allora. Cathrine was jealous of the fact of them spending time alone together. Though she knew Gawain was a good man and this must be important to him.

"Gawain we both know that I possess no item you need for your mission. What are you actually wanting from me?" Allora questioned him.

"Leon persists on heading to the tomb," Gawain answered.

"And?"

"I don't believe him to be ready."

"What do you expect from me?"

"Talk him out of it, he will listen to you."

"Then why did you give him the blade?"

"I don't know. It felt like the time was right."

"What a strange response."

Gawain glared back at her, "Why is that so strange?"

"You say he is not ready, yet you have given him the blade. Yet here you stand wishing for me to guide him elsewhere. And you of all people know that I cannot. His destiny is set in stone, there is no changing that. Perhaps Gawain you are the one that's not ready. Have you thought of that?"

"Perhaps I am done witnessing needless bloodshed."

"Like it or not Gawain your destiny is intertwined with his. Where he goes you will follow without even knowing it. If he fails it will be because of your weakness not his own."

"What must I do?"

"Find the Gawain of old, that is my only advice to you."

Five days later when landfall was made it was hard to believe that anything dangerous would be lying in wait like Allora had warned. Rolling green lush hills went as far as the eye could see. There was a large patch of trees off to the right and overly large boulders off to the left. Straight ahead was nothing but open range. Also wild horses ran up and down the hills along with other creatures they had never seen before. The land was beautiful and lush offering them a false feeling of peace.

"Which way?" Jeffery asked.

"Not into the woods," Aurelius answered.

"Why not?" Leladda questioned.

"A strong elven magic blocks our way."

"Can't you allow us passage?"

Aurelius shook his head, "That I cannot do."

"Are you not of elven blood?" Jeffery responded.

"Yes, but different elves have their own kind of magic. Even if I tried, I couldn't bring down the barrier."

"Why put up a barrier?"

Leon walked up beside them, "Why else? To keep us out." He walked on ahead ignoring the wooded area all together.

"Where are you going?" Aurelius was the one asking the questions this time around.

Leon stopped and turned his head slightly to look back at him, "The path we must take," he said and began walking on ahead for a second time.

Gawain and Catherine walked past them as well, Catherine had the same stern look on her face as usual. And Gawain was chuckling to himself. Even he knew not to question Leon when he had his mind set on something. This time the young man that he knew so well was different. He was more precise with his actions, more confident in his decisions and didn't second guess himself.

Gawain was proud to see that his former student had come so far. It was a shame that he wasn't there to help him cope with the things that had transpired over the last couple of years. Surely it wasn't easy on him being a captive on a pirate ship. Knowing that he had a mission to accomplish to stop King Alistair and Caine's evil plans.

He thought of the torture Leon had to of endured at the hands of that twisted man, Bosch. And how much strength it must have taken to resist giving out the information the Captain sought. Things like that change a person and not for the good. Leon seemed to be handling it well, but for how long.

"Where are you taking us?" Leladda's question snapped Gawain out of the trance. He too wished to know where exactly Leon was taking them and what to expect.

"Bhim Garohm," Leon answered.

"Never heard of such a place."

"I prefer we didn't go there," Bosch said.

"We have no choice," Leon responded.

"Could someone tell me about this place?"

"The place is an underground city built by the Dwarves," Gawain explained.

"And those smelly little guys hate everything and everyone," Bosch spate.

"Or possibly they just hate you," Aurelius smirked.

"Perhaps."

"Then we will have at least one thing in common with them," Gawain added.

"All joking aside, you know they will never speak with us," said Aurelius.

"Don't need them too."

"Then why go?"

"We need certain weapons and armor made for us if we hope to survive inside the Tomb."

"Like they will aid us."

"One will."

"Who?"

"Mokgrith Orecloak will aid us," Leon answered.

"What makes this Dwarf so special?" Aurelius questioned him again.

"He forges armor and weapons out of magical items."

"Forging those kinds of things are forbidden amongst his people."

"That's why the blacksmith will aid us," Leon replied. "He's very proud of his handy work and we can use that to our advantage."

"How do you know all of this?" Gawain chimed in.

"A little birdy told me."

"You mean the dragon?"

"Not this time."

"Then who?"

"You will just have to trust me," Leon said with a smile on his face that no one could see.

"I hope this doesn't blow up in our faces," Gawain whispered to Cathrine.

"This is his quest now Gawain," Cathrine whispered back. "He must do this with or without you. Whether you believe in him or not is of no concern."

There was one overly large hill that was straight ahead. Leon had informed them that over this hill was the cave that would lead them to the dwarven city. At the top was the end of the beautiful landscape, down below was a dark greyish dank place. Filled with jagged stones and some kind of strange fog.

Allora spoke of dangers, this would be the place that would provide such things. But something else could be seen stirring down below, it looked like large groups of men. It clearly wasn't Dwarfs they are rarely seen out in the open. Though a foul smell filled the air that told a story of what really laid in wait.

"Umbramen," Gawain spate. "I would rather have dealt with a Rock Giant than those blasted things."

"What are they?" Leladda asked.

"Not very knowledgeable for a princess," said Bosch.

"This is the first time I've been out of the castle," she responded.

"Pampered."

"More like a prisoner."

"Quiet," Gawain hissed. "We do not need them to hear or see us."

"What's the plan?" Aurelius asked.

"Ask Leon," Gawain responded. Leon shot Gawain a look of anger or possibly confusion. "It is your quest to finish. My attention is on doing the job that I was paid to do."

The young man looked back down the hill, he was thinking about the safest path to stay away from the Umbramen. That many of them gathered around in one place was unheard of. Most of the time they ran in small tribes or packs. Never would they come together to form such a large group unless something or someone had brought them here. Leon pointed out, "There is a path off to the left, protected by a line of boulders. Not sure if that was put there by Dwarves, but it is the safest passage," he explained.

"Are you not afraid of them smelling us?" Bosch questioned, best be on the side of caution.

"No," Leon answered. "The Dwarves put off an odor stronger than ours. If it is safe for them then it should be safe for us as well."

"That is true," Bosch agreed. "You have a keen eye and you're smarter than I gave you credit for."

"I don't need your praises," Leon huffed.

"Not praises, just stating the obvious."

"Let's go," Leon demanded. "Get down the hill quickly and stay close to the boulders. Most important of all stay quiet."

The group made their way down the hill as quickly as possible without drawing attention towards them. Leladda's sight was drawn towards the Umbramen. At first glance they looked human, wearing ragged armor and carried strange looking weapons. Their eyes however were black as coal. The skin on their bones was wrinkled and saggy, and they spoke a weird language that she couldn't grasp.

Perhaps these things were once human but no longer. Evil had transformed them, made what was once man a pawn in the war for power. A shame they couldn't realize it before it was too late. Leon led the way, there were a few times it seemed the Umbramen had noticed them but went back to what they were doing. One slip up and they would be dead where they stood, a feast for the Umbramen.

The cave to the dwarven city was right in front of them, all they had to do was make it there alive. It was a good distance away and the Umbramen were around every corner. Leon lifted his hand in the air, "Cover your eyes," he warned. He said a few words and a bright light erupted causing the creatures to scream in pain and anger. They swung their weapons wildly accidently killing the others around them.

"Run!" Leon shouted.

Inside the cave Gawain was quick to question what Leon had done, "What kind of spell was that?"

"A spell of blinding," Leladda answered instead.

"I don't remember teaching him that," Gawain replied.

"He learned it from watching me," she said. "Not sure how he could pick up on it in such a short time. It took me years of training to learn that spell. And yet he made it look easy, and even took it a step further by widening the area it could reach."

"You still haven't heard a word I have said. I am not like you or the others," Leon responded as he walked past. "The city is just up ahead let's keep moving."

On the sides of the cave walls bulbs glowed a bright blue leading the way. Must have been some sort of magic or special tool the Dwarves used to give them light. It was a magnificent sight when they first gazed upon the great dwarven city. The Dwarves were very handy with hammers and were able to build stone buildings and houses inside the cave.

It was amazing to see an actual city built underground, with lights and everything else you would see in a normal human city. The group was approached by three Dwarves. Two wore battle armor and carried axes, while the one leading the way was much older. He was dressed in certain clothing and walked with aid from his cane.

"Humans are not welcome here," one of them said in a stern voice

The eldest raised his hand, "There is no reason for such harsh words," he said. "Forgive him, some still have yet to let go of their hatred. My name is Thutot Blunthorn. I am one of the three elders of the great city of Bhim Garohm. What may I ask are you doing here?"

"We are seeking out, Mokgrith Orecloak," Leon answered.

The elder seemed taken aback by the response, "Is there a reason you seek him out?" He questioned. "Try not to lie to me young man, I can tell when you're being honest." Leon figured the truth would be easier and explained everything that had led up to that point. "I see, so the prophecy has come true. Mokgrith stays on the far end of the city, his experiments have him hated by many. Remember not all here like humans or Elves for that matter. Keep to yourselves and leave when you are done."

Even though they walked away Leon could still feel the presence of the Dwarven guards. As he suspected they would not be alone on this search for Mokgrith. The group walked towards the far end of town as directed. Bosch kept his eyes open, paranoia was taken hold of the pirate captain. It was clear to the others that Bosch was nervous, and it was the first time they had seen a look of fear in his eyes.

What had he done here in his past that he didn't want to come back? Or perhaps he was afraid of someone that lived here and hoped he wouldn't run into them. Whatever it was, clearly the so called fearless captain was scared for his life. When they made it to the outskirts of town Bosch breathed a sigh of relief.

"Let's knock on his door, do what we have to do and get the hell out of here," Bosch said.

"What has you so worked up?" Aurelius asked.

"Nothing, nothing at all," he nervously laughed. "We need to hurry and get back to my ship is all."

"Who did you double cross?"

"That is none of your concern."

"It is of my concern if being with you will land us all in a lot of trouble."

Bosch didn't want to share too much information so he gave up what he was willing to share with them. "Let's just say I made some ill advised trading here. I got what I wanted and they, well they didn't exactly get what they expected."

"You cheated them."

"More or less."

"Forget about that," Leon said. He walked up to the small stone house and knocked on the door. The door creaked open and standing before them was a dwarven man. He was of medium height which meant he was taller than normal. His hair was long and black with streaks of grey, his beard was long, all the way down to his large belly.

"Humans," he grunted. "What do you want?"

"I was told to seek you out," Leon answered.

"By who?"

"The water dragon."

"A dragon talked with a human?" He laughed, "I've never heard such ridiculousness."

"It's true." Leon reached into his bag and pulled out a weird dark purple crystal.

The dwarven man's eyes widened, "Where did you get that?"

"Where did you get that?" Gawain questioned as well.

"I borrowed it from the amazon women," Leon responded.

"You stole it," said Gawain.

Leon shrugged, "Borrowed, stole it. Doesn't matter I was told to take it."

"Seems the boy has a little bit of pirate in him," Bosch said with an amused look on his face.

"What would you have me do with that?" The Dwarven man asked.

"I need to know if your name is Mokgrith Orecloak first," said Leon.

"Who else would I be?"

"Good." He unsheathed his blade and handed it over to Mokgrith, "I need you to remove the jewel on the bottom of the hilt and replace it with this one."

"This is one of the legendary blades," Mokgrith gasped.

"That is correct," Leon replied.

"It still wouldn't be enough to bring back its powers."

"Though it would be a step in the right direction."

"And what makes you think I will help you?"

Leon smiled, "You're a blacksmith and one of the best at what you do. I doubt you can walk away from bringing back life to such a wonderful weapon."

Mokgrith thought about what the young human had said. It was a blacksmith's duty to breath life into his craft. And a blade such as that would put his name in the history books for many years to come. "Come inside," he insisted. Inside his home, he explained that he would be willing to help them for a price. He wanted a certain item from within the tomb.

Back in the time before the great war, Dwarves, Elves and Humans lived in perfect harmony together. Each had a specific set of skills, and Dwarves were extremely talented blacksmiths. One though was better than all the rest. He even created one of the best smithy hammers in all the lands, it was of legends. It was said that the hammer could make magical items and weapons look easy.

"You want a blacksmith hammer?" Leon asked. Mokgrith nodded, "How will we know which is the right one?" He questioned.

"When you gaze upon it you will know."

"You have a deal." Leon held out his hand and Mokgrith took hold of his wrist and Leon did the same to him. The agreement was sealed, and the blacksmith took the blade and the purple stone into the next room. He insisted the others stay put, he needed his full concentration to complete his work.

Mokgrith worked hard and steady over the flames in which he used to shape and mold the jewel. The sounds of his trusty hammer could be heard banging away as he chipped away at the newly formed jewel. Sweat dripped from his brow as he stood there admiring his work. Now it was time to see if it would fit. Though he knew that wasn't going to be much of a worry.

After hours of waiting Mokgrith returned with the blade as promised and handed it back to Leon. "Tell me young man. Do you know how to restore the blades' power?"

"I do not," Leon answered. "Though I was told it would become clear to me once at the tomb."

"You know about the blade?" Gawain interrupted.

"Why would I not? My Dwarven ancestors helped to create the weapons of power."

"Do you know how to restore the blade to its former glory?" Gawain asked.

"Only the chosen one can accomplish this feat, and seeing how you have the blade that must be you," said Mokgrith.

"That seems to be the case not that I like it," Leon responded. "Tell me what I must do."

"If you get lucky enough to make it deep within the tomb alive. You must face a warrior quiet like yourself. Best him and he will provide what you need to restore the blade."

"That's it?"

"Nothing is ever that easy," Mokgrith responded. "You must become one with the blade to best him."

"How do I accomplish that?"

"That you will have to figure out on your own."

"What if I fail?"

Mokgrith shrugged, "The blade will take your life."

Leon lightly chuckled, "Had a feeling it would be something like that," he replied.

"I refuse to let that happen!" Gawain blurted out.

Mokgrith cared not for humans, not even for the chosen one. It was there kind that dabbled in magic they didn't understand. Which was what created the Dark Knights and brought chaos into the world. They are the ones that caused a rift between the races and brought upon the Great War.

Evil ones, chosen one, it didn't matter to him. The world could fall into darkness again and yet he wouldn't care. His people would be protected regardless of the outcome, or so he had thought. The only reason he was helping them was for the greater good of his kind.

"I don't care what you do, just make sure you hold up your end of the deal," said Mokgrith. "See your way out, I have more work to be done." He turned and disappeared back down to his work room.

"Leon I forbid you to try and become one with that damn blade," Gawain huffed.

"It is the path I must take," Leon responded.

"At the sake of your own life?" Gawain questioned. "That is foolhardy."

"Call it what you will," said Leon. "I will see this through to the end."

"You are too important alive."

"Why because I am the chosen one?"

"That and," Gawain paused.

"And what?" Leon barked.

"I don't want to see you die," Gawain answered. "Is that what you want to hear? There has been too much death. And has it been worth it? No it hasn't! Look at where all this leads us, to our deaths. Don't throw your life away as well."

"That choice is not yours to make," said Leon. "This curse is mine to bare. You gave up in the fight against the darkness, I have not. If I die, so be it."

CHAPTER NINE

THE CHAMBERLAIN MAKES HIS MOVE

Ballard was a cunning and vile man that wanted only one thing, power and riches. And he was willing to hurt and destroy anyone that could stop his plans. Or he would use a certain King to unknowingly aid in quest to fulfill his darkest of desires. The old book that Alistair had given him over a year ago had proved useful.

He had learned about things that no normal human could know or understand. It was doubtful that even that idiot king realized what he held in his hands. And so willing to give it away just to get rid of a small thorn in his side. Ballard had become more than a man, he used a forbidden spell that kept him from aging.

But it came at a cost, he had to constantly consume human souls for the spell to keep working. Though in his mind it was a small price to pay to ensure his future would be intact. He also learned of something else that may be of use to him. It was a blood red jewel of the dark order said to be buried in the kingdom of Picolum.

The kingdom was full of weak minded fools that trotted around preaching peace and love. It would be an easy win seeing how they didn't believe in violence. They probably had no idea such a relic dwelled deep within their catacombs. Now it was time to place the seed of deception inside Alistair's mind.

Ballard didn't have to request an audience with the king, he was welcome inside the king's chamber anytime he wanted. "Ballard, to what do I owe this visit?" He responded to the sight of the Chamberlain. Alistair was more agitated than usual which could play into Ballard's favor.

"King Alistair." Ballard bowed.

"Cut the shit," Alistair grunted. "I assume you want something. What may that be?"

"Guess we're skipping the pleasantries," Ballard responded. "I have a proposition for you, if you're interested."

"I'm listening."

"You would do best to wage war against Picolum and take that kingdom for yourself."

"Why would I do that?" Alistair questioned.

"Think of the resources you would gain," Ballard replied.

"Such as?"

"Herbs and medicine to aid your wounded."

"I have the Dark Knights they do not need such things."

"True," Ballard replied, he had known the words he must say to bring the king to his side. "Think of the people, how will they see things if you constantly use the Dark Knights to win battles. And the Knights that are willing to die for you. When you do need them their morale will be lowered if you always act as though you don't." His words were well thought out and precise. And rung true with Alistair and his plans for a one world kingdom with him in charge.

"That would not go in my favor if that were to happen," said Alistair. "If I did this what would be in it for you?"

Ballard couldn't very well tell him of the jewel, however he could tell him of what could be done with some of the plants. "Some of the plants are not just used for its healing powers," he stated. "They can also be made into a powerful poison. The same that was used with that powerful weapon a couple of years ago."

"Doesn't sound useful to you."

"Useful for the Kingdom not me."

"Explain."

"Let's say a kingdom is strong even for us. We unleash a poison upon them and they become weak, too weak to even put up a fight. Or if you wish to turn neighboring kingdom's against one another. See where I am going with this?" Ballard smiled gleefully.

"And how would you assume we handle the situation?"

"Like I said we wage war against them."

Alistair shook his head, "I am about to wage war against the world. Wasting resources on Picolum would be foolhardy on my part. Come up with another way and I shall agree."

"Then lend me a handful of you knights that should suffice."

"What would be your plan of action?"

Ballard smiled, "Merely talk is all that would be acquired," he said.

"Under one condition."

"Name it."

"Start making the poison right away."

"As you wish my lord," Ballard bowed before turning to walk away.

It was a two day ride to the Kingdom Of Picolum. Ballard knew there would be no need for a fight. And the knights with him were just for show of force if necessary. If he played his cards correctly he would use fear to win over the King and Queen. And the promise of protection from the good King Alistair if they agreed to be under his banner of the one world order.

And if they refused, he had other means to enforce the new laws of the land upon them. Picolum, wasn't one of the greater kingdoms but held the artifact he sought. The kingdom looked more like one large farm than anything. The herbs and other foreign plants were grown as far as the eye could see. There were a few houses here and there but nothing that stood out. And the castle looked more like an old run down church of light.

Why would someone hide an artifact of power here in these parts? Ballard thought to himself. Perhaps this was once a thriving kingdom of old. Destroyed in the Great War, and forgotten by time until these herbalists built their own kingdom here. He doubted they even knew what they had stumbled upon.

"What would you have us do?" One of the knights asked.

"Follow me to the castle," Ballard answered.

"Why have you brought us here?"

"That is none of your concern," Ballard hissed.

"It does if it concerns my men's safety."

"You answer to me, that's all you need to know."

"I answer only to King Alistair and Sir Caine." The knight belted.

"King Alistair gave you specific orders to obey my commands!" Ballard retorted.

"For now," he responded. "But know if you cross any lines it will be your head."

"Your threat is duly noted," said Ballard. "And will be reported to your king upon our return."

Ballard and the knights didn't have time to dismount from their horses as they were quickly greeted by a man dressed like a person of royalty. "What do I owe this visit from the Knights Of Valor?" He asked.

"First I would like to know who is greeting us?" Ballard replied.

"My name is George. And yours?"

"I am Chamberlain to King Alistair, the name is Ballard. Are you the King?"

"Yes I am the King. Again why are you here?"

"To offer protection."

"Protection from what?"

"The Dark Knights of course," Ballard answered.

"No one can protect us from them," George replied. "Not even the mighty Alistair."

"Oh but you're wrong. Alistair when strong enough, can drive off the Dark Knights."

"Is this true?" King George gasped.

"It is very true."

"At what cost?"

"We want half of you herbs and other plants."

"Will we be paid?"

"Name a price," replied Ballard.

"Three hundred silver every other cycle," George said.

"How about two hundred?" Asked Ballard.

"Seems fair enough. What else do you require of us?"

"Passage into the catacombs."

"Even if I suggest against it?"

"Do not worry, we are very capable of handling ourselves."

"What if I refuse?"

"We leave and when the time comes there will be no one to help you. And you and your people will surely perish."

"If you promise to protect my people then we have a deal."

"I promise." Though Ballard could care less about King George and his people. If they died tomorrow it would matter not, he would have what he sought either way. And of course the ground would still be fertile to grow the plants with or without humans living there.

"We will join you," George held out his hand and Ballard reached out and gripped his wrist.

"Good," Ballard smiled, "Tell us how we can get to the catacombs please."

"Down the old well at the center of town. It's the only way to get inside the catacombs. Be warned though, the ones that have gone down never made it back up."

A warning from some peace loving King wasn't about to sway Ballard from entering the catacombs. Though the thought of dying in such a place did make him rethink his plan. That is why I brought a handful of Knights with me, he thought to himself. This wasn't a journey he would make but they would make for him.

"Gather your things Captain, I have a job for you," Ballard said.

"If you think you are sending me and my men down into the catacombs your crazy."

"This is not for me but for King Alistair." Ballard was good at weaving a web of deception. "Now that we have gained the townspeople's trust. I can tell you the real reason we are here."

"Which is?"

"To retrieve a great artifact of power," Ballard replied. "It will be of great aid to Alistair's mission. Think what will await for the ones that accomplish this feat. I will not take credit, but you shall. You might even be given the rank of second in command to Lord Caine himself."

"What am I looking for?"

Ballard had the golden tongue indeed, "I knew you would see things my way," he said. After a brief exchange of words explaining the mission at hand and what the artifact looked like to the knights. Ballard sent them on their way.

He waited anxiously for their return, the thought of holding the artifact brought on an excitement he couldn't explain. Hours had passed and no sign of the knights. If they failed, what would be the next move he could make. Perhaps he could hire some mercenaries to enter the catacombs. Yes, that would be the next attempt to get his hands on the jewel.

He went to walk away until he heard screams coming from inside the well. It seemed the men had survived after all, but something was chasing them. Ballard watched one of the knights climb out of the well. It was the captain of the guard, he had removed his helmet and tossed it to the side. He was bent over heaving for air, trickles of blood dripped from his forehead.

"Did you get it?" Ballard shouted.

The knight threw a piece of cloth over in front of Ballard's feet. He reached down and picked it up. Unraveling what was inside the cloth. His eyes widened and a smile stretched across his face. His mission was a success.

"Is that what you were after?"

"It was," Ballard responded. He now had to figure out a way to dispose of the knight. He couldn't very well let the news of the artifact reach King Alistair.

"I lost my men down there, I hope it was worth it."

"It was worth it," Ballard assured him. "King Alistair will be proud, and your men will be honored as well." The knight was weak and battle worn. He had no idea what was about to happen next, even if he did, he wouldn't be quick enough to defend himself. Ballard pulled a small blade, unbeknownst to the knight.

"What is our next move?"

"Unfortunately for you, death is the next move." Ballard plunged the blade into the knights neck. His eyes had a look of disbelief in them, betrayed by one of his own. Ballard pushed the man backwards into the well. He waited until he heard the thud of the body hitting the ground below. Ballard simply wiped the blood off the blade and walked away with no remorse.

CHAPTER TEN

THE BLACK KNIGHT, FRIEND OR FOE?

Ellyn was sitting alone by the fire looking up at the night sky. The stars above shined brightly. Most of the time if you studied them closely they will lead the way. Or so they say, but she had a hard time believing in such stories. She had stared at the stars many many nights and yet got no closer to finding her brother.

Ellyn went to raise up but was held down, it was the knight from before. He covered her mouth and motioned for her to stay quiet. She still did not feel threatened by him. Ellyn nodded to let him know she understood and would not scream.

"What are you doing here?" She whispered. Ellyn waited for a response but he said nothing. "Do you not speak?" Again no response from the knight. "If you're not going to talk, you might as well leave."

"Most of the time I do not speak with others," he said. The knights voice was deep and husky and somewhat distorted. He must have been using a spell to keep his real voice from being heard.

"Why are you in our camp?"

"To speak with you."

"What do you want with me?"

"To give information."

"About?"

"Your brother."

It was the first that she had heard of her brother in over a year. "What information do you have? Is he hurt? Or is he dead?" You could see the panic flood over her face.

"Your brother is still alive."

"Thank the gods." She breathed a sigh of relief.

"Are you ready to listen now?"

"I grant you permission to speak."

"I need not your permission to speak princess," he responded smuggly. "Your arrogance is well noted. Though this isn't about you is it? This is about your brother, and he is in need of your help."

"Tell me about my brother damnit!"

"He's been placed in the dungeons," the knight answered. "He will be executed in three days time."

"Where? Why?" Ellyn gasped.

The Black Knight held up his hand, "Don't worry, I have a way to save him. That's why I came to you, it's your brother and I knew you would help me save him," he explained.

"There must be a reason you want to help him."

"That will have to wait for another time," he said. "Meet me in the next town. If you find an inn called the Three Horse's you will be in the right place. We can speak more of the situation there and only there."

Ellyn went to speak but like a dream the knight had vanished and she found herself staring strangely at Lance and Shena. The sun was up and Lance was cooking some kind of rodent while Shena was packing the saddle bags. Ellyn felt groggy and was unsure of what had happened, it was night moments ago while she was talking to that knight.

And now the sun was up and she found herself watching Lance and Shena with no words to speak. Shena glanced over at Ellyn, "Look who finally decided to join the land of the living," she said with a smile. Though she noticed the princess wasn't acting like her normal self, "Are you feeling well?"

Ellyn tried to shake the cobwebs from her head, "Just confused is all," she responded.

"Well we did just barely survive a battle," said Shena. "I think we're all just a bit tired."

"It's not that."

"Then what?"

"It was night time and I was talking with that knight that saved our lives," Ellyn explained. "Next I know it's daytime and here we are."

"He must have invaded your dreams," Lance interrupted, as he brought some food over to them.

"Not the time for jokes," Shena snarled.

"Who said I was joking?"

"How can someone invade another's dreams?" Ellyn questioned.

"Good question," Shena added. "Explain."

"Here in these lands there are some that can use magic to invade dreams," he answered. "Though I thought only the Elves could use that kind of magic. And I don't see them using any type of armor that humans wear."

"That kind of magic exists?" Shena responded.

"Elves are one with the elements, they know stuff that we can't even phantom," Lance replied. "Did he say anything of importance?"

"He said my brother was going to be executed in three days," Ellyn answered. "And that he would explain more if we sought him out at an inn called the Three Horse's."

"I know of that place," said Lance. "It's in the small town of Larken. Not even a half a day ride from here."

"Sounds suspicious to me," Shena spate. "I don't like it."

"Doesn't matter, if Rin is in trouble then we must find out," said Ellyn.

Shena sighed, "Very well," she responded. "If Prince Rin is in trouble we shall help him."

"Then I shall accompany you," Lance spoke up.

"We don't need a knight in shining armor to save us," replied Shena coldly.

"You have my blade regardless."

"No use trying to stop you."

Like Lance had said the small town wasn't that far away, and they made their way there before noon. It wasn't much of a town, more like a drinking spot for knights and mercenaries to spend their gold in exchange for a good time. Taverns lined the dirt streets but one stood out more than the others.

The building itself was the tallest in town, it was bright white and easily drew attention to itself. There was a handle full knights passed out, leaning up against the building. All while thieves quietly snuck around picking their pockets. As much as they wished this wasn't the place, the symbol above the doors was of three horses. Lance gave a smile and entered first, Ellyn and Shena followed in pursuit.

Inside the inn was no better than the outside possibly worse. It smelled of booze and tobacco. On top of that it was loud and packed full of different types of people, mainly knights from other countries. Scantily dressed women were hanging all over the men. It was hard to watch, as Ellyn thought men of honor should be out fighting for and protecting the people of the lands.

"Sickening," Ellyn grunted.

"Despicable," Shena added.

"What has you ladies so worked up?" Lance questioned.

"Look around you," Shena snapped. "This is not how knights act."

Lance looked around the room not seeing a problem with what he was witnessing, "I don't see a problem with any of this."

Ellyn glared at him, "You condone this?" She bellowed.

"Keep it down, you're drawing unwanted attention." They turned to see the knight wearing black armor standing before them. "We will talk over in that corner away from the others."

"Now can we talk?" Ellyn asked.

"Hold one." He scanned the room making sure there were no eyes upon them. "It would seem no one has an interest in us which is good."

"How did you get into our camp last night without me knowing?" Shena questioned out of curiosity.

"I did not enter your camp."

"Then how did you talk with the princess?"

"I entered her dreams."

"Only Elves can use that kind of magic," Lance said.

"Not true. Anyone can learn that type of magic if they're strong enough."

"Why do you hide your true voice from us?" Shena asked another question.

"How did you learn such a spell?" Lance asked.

"These questions are getting under my skin," the knight responded. "This day is not about me but her brother." Referring to Ellyn.

"He's right," said Ellyn. "Where is he being held and what can we do to save him?"

"King Aidan is the one that has your brother."

"What?!" She gasped. "For what reason is he being held?"

"For treason against the crown."

"That's ridiculous!"

"King Aidan found out your involvement in helping destroy his pet project."

"That has nothing to do with my brother."

"In his mind it does. The King is hoping to draw you out with this information."

"How do you know this?"

"I was hired by Aidan to find you, give you this information and lead you back to his kingdom so he could execute you both."

"Why should we trust you?" Ellyn questioned.

"You can't," he responded.

"Then why are you offering to help us?"

"It would be beneficial for both of us if King Aidan was out of the way."

"That's why you need our help."

"It is," he replied. "Aidan is a power crazed man that needs to be stopped at all costs. Will you help or not?"

"If it will save my brother count me in. What about you Shena?"

"You're going to do this regardless of what I say. Someone needs to be there to protect you."

"I already offered my blade," said Lance. "I need a good fight to keep the blood pumping."

"Then it is settled," the man said.

"If we're going to work together, I need to know what to call you."

"You can call me Rowan for the time being."

"I take it that's not your real name," Shena responded.

"Names are not important."

"I guess that will work for now."

With Rowan leading the way the group had made it to the Kingdom Of Odrela right on the day Rin was to be executed. Rowan had a plan but it was as simple as using them as bait. To many guards around for such a simple strategy as that to work. They were to dress as normal townspeople and blend in with the crowd.

Rowan would hide in the bell tower and use his skill with a bow and special arrows to help fight off reinforcements. All Ellyn had to do was be patient enough to wait for the signal to attack. Drums were heard playing on beat with one another as four prisoners were being led out. One of the four prisoners was for sure Prince Rin.

There was no grand stage just a guillotine in the middle of the town square. The overly sized executioner stood there waiting to do his one and only job. Release the sharp metal blade that will part the mens head from their shoulders in bloody fashion. The prisoners we lined up one behind the other.

Aidan stood off in the distance away from the crowd that had gathered. Perhaps he hated his people or they hated him, or both were the case. He stood and gave a speech that a King would normally give at an execution. The townspeople were booing him while the knights protected their leader.

The first man that was led to the guillotine had to have been no older than Ellyn. He didn't look to be scared, instead he had a look of defiance and pride. Ellyn wanted to save this young man but was held back by Lance and Shena. They stood there and watched as the blade was released and his head rolled forward followed by a crimson red liquid.

Moments later another was led to the guillotine and executed like the man before him. Ellyn was horrified by what she was witnessing, she had no idea the brutality of this form of justice. When it was Rin's turn to be executed Ellyn wanted to rush by his side. The wait for the signal to save her brother felt like an eternity.

An arrow zipped through the air and hit the executioner square between the eyes before he could even touch the rope. That was the signal they had been waiting for. Ellyn, Lance and Shean rushed through the crowd to aid Rin. Aidan had seen the attempt to save the last prisoner and knew exactly who was attempting this prison break. He demanded that his knights kill them all.

Another arrow flew through the air and hit the ground causing an explosion that killed a handful of knights. Explosive arrows were not unheard of but very rare. Moments later another arrow hit the ground followed by another explosion. That was their que to get the hell out of there. Thanks to Rowan they managed to save Rin with little to no effort at all.

Rowan didn't leave with the others, he had another agenda on his mind. The Black Knight went for Aidan himself, somehow he knew the layout of the castle. And waited for the king to return to his chambers, when he did Rowan made his move.

"You betrayed me!" Aidan belted.

"Smart."

"Should have known better than trust in you."

"I did as you asked. Wsa this not what you wanted?"

"You dirty rat!"

"Is that any way to speak to the man that's about to end your life?"

Aidan drew his blade, "You think it will be that easy?"

Rowan unsheathed his sword, "Your skills are no match for mine."

Aidan swung his blade at Rowan, the knight dodged the attack with little to no effort. "Not bad," said Aidan.

"Is that the best you've got?"

Those words infuriated King Aidan and he went on a full out attack. He slashed the blade upward connecting with nothing but air. Then again he brought the blade down back down at Rowan's head. The knight used his sword to knock the attack away. Aidan kept continuing with the onslaught. Mounting attack after attack, each more intense than the last.

Yet as hard as he tried he couldn't land a single blow against the knight. Aidan was getting fatigued, the attacks he was using started to take a toll on his body. He was infusing his body with magic to make himself quicker and stronger. Still he couldn't match the knight in black armor's quickness.

"How can I not land a single strike?!" Aidan hissed.

"I told you, your skills are no match for mine," he replied. "Not even the magic you use can aid you in this fight."

The king went to swing his blade again, Rowan held up his hand and said a few words. Aidan was surprised when he was stopped in his tracks and could no longer move. "What have you done to me?" He angrily asked.

"I grew tired of your weak attacks," said Rowan. "So I placed a spell of binding on you."

"Why are you doing this to me?"

"You've been a thorn in someone's side and they sent me here to deal with you on a personal level."

"Why save the prince?"

"Needed a distraction."

"Whatever they are paying you I can double, no triple it," Aidan insisted. "I will even let you become the captain of the guard. How does that sound?"

"Like a man that knows he's about to die."

"Damn you!" The King screamed out. "My people will have your head for this!"

"Your people won't even know you're gone." Rowan removed his helmet showing his true identity to the king.

"You," Aidan gasped. "Now I understand."

"King Alistair sends his regards." Rowan swung his blade through the air lopping Aidan's head from his shoulders. The knight put his helmet back on and reached down to pick up the head of Aidan. Placing it in a small brown cloth bag.

CHAPTER ELEVEN

CAINE READIES THE RESISTANCE

Caine had found himself standing outside of the resistance hideout. Apparently they had no idea he was outside or they didn't view him as a threat. Or perhaps this was a test to see if Caine would be brave enough or stupid enough to walk on inside. Sure enough Caine walked on inside, if things went wrong he wasn't worried about it.

"I had a feeling you would be back," Stilfadr greeted.

"Waited for me I see," Caine laughed.

"I am no fool. The first time you were here it was for a reason. Am I correct?"

"What if I were the enemy?"

"You would be dead where you stood." Stilfadr looked in all directions. Making sure to point out his men that stood in the shadows waiting for a signal to attack.

"Smart man."

"Keeps you alive."

"That's true enough."

"Care to answer my first question?"

"You're correct in your assumption," Caine agreed. "I do need something from you."

"And what was your name again?"

"You already know the answer."

"Remind me," Stilfadr smirked.

"Shawn, and no, last names are not important. Now will you tell your men to lower their weapons?"

"Not going to happen," Stilfadr replied. "What is it you need from us?"

"Your help."

"Our help," Stilfadr laughed. "What makes you think we will help someone we don't even know?'

"Then why did you save me?"

"It was the right thing to do."

"So is this," he pleaded.

"Convince me."

"This is the reason I was running from those knights." Caine or now Shawn reached under the breastplate of his armor and pulled out a rolled up parchment paper.

"Why is that so important they were willing to kill you to get it back?"

"These are blueprints to King Alistair's castle."

"How did you get a hold of them?"

"I stole them."

"For who?"

"Does it matter?"

"And what would you like us to do?"

"Help me put an end to his reign of terror."

"You're crazy!" Stilfadr bellowed.

Shawn tossed the rolled up parchment over to Stilfadr, "I am a man of action. What are they?"

"Even if this got us inside the castle, I don't have the manpower to pull off such a mission."

"You will with my help."

“You’ve been planning this move for a long time.”

“Not me, but the ones that have paid for my services.”

“And who are they?” Stilfadr questioned.

“That will be answered in time,” said Shawn. “I will give you a month to decide. I expect an answer upon my return.”

“And what of these?” He referred to the blueprints in hand.

“Keep them, just in case.” Shawn turned and walked away, leaving Stilfadr to decide his own fate in this twisted game of power.

CHAPTER TWELVE

ALISTAIR LOSES A PIECE OF HIMSELF TO THE BLADE

Caine made his return to the castle of Drasal after being away for three long months. He hoped the blade hadn't taken too much of the old Alistair away in his absence. Caine had a way of keeping things under control. Not allowing the cursed blade to drive Alistair towards the brink of insanity. Though with his plan in motion, it was time to let the crazed Alistair loose on the lands.

If the king's mind wasn't already decaying it would be after what Caine was going to tell him. A simple nudge to convince Alistair it was time to wage war on the rest of the lands and bring out the full power of the blade. Once that was accomplished all the king would be is a man full of hate and rage possessed by the blade.

Though all of this was brought on by Alistair himself when he became a puppet to his own greed and obsession. As Cain had been relentlessly searching for a way to begin his plan for years. Which started the day he had joined the Academy. Once he learned that Alistair had acquired a certain ancient book. He took it as a sign from the gods that his destiny was near and joined Alistair in his dirty deeds.

Not a single time did Alistair suspect Cain had his own

intentions. For he was too busy assuming that with the power of the blade he would become a god. Rule the world under one banner, his own. Caine approached Alistair and quickly noticed that the good king seemed a little on edge. He was somewhat twitchy and looked over his shoulder like he was paranoid.

Caine fought back the urge to grin, clearly the blade was wanting to take a life. And it was driving Alistair to the point of madness if he didn't drown his bloodlust that the blade was making him feel. "Are you feeling well my King?" Caine asked.

"Better now that you've returned," said Alistair.

"What about the Chamberlain? Has he not been by your side?"

"He has been tending to other pressing matters."

"Have you not made your move yet?" Caine questioned. "The rest of the Kingdoms will not liberate themselves."

"I have been deciding on who I should extend the olive branch too."

"Olive branch?" Caine replied with a confused look on his face. "Peace is not the way. You have to strike fear into their hearts for them to understand or they will laugh you off like some kind of joke. What has happened to the ruthless Alistair that killed King Edward and took the crown for himself? What happened to the man that tamed the cursed blade and burned down the Academy?"

"I don't feel like myself lately."

"Are you feeling regret? Have you succumbed to the human emotions that you claim as a weakness?"

"I'm not sure what I feel."

"It must be the blade," said Caine.

"The cursed blade has made me weak hasn't it?" Alistair questioned.

"It has."

"But I did everything correctly. What has gone wrong?"

"Have you given a piece of yourself to the blade as Zerius suggested?"

"I thought that would be pointless as I have control over the sword."

Caine sighed, "You must decide what part of yourself you wish to give over to the blade," he said. "Or it will not recognize you as its owner."

Alistair hated what he was feeling so the choice was simple, he would offer up what made him human, the ability to feel. The King closed his eyes and offered that part of himself to the dark blade. A dark aura surrounded Alistair's body and the blade awakened once more. This time a voice whispered to him telling him it was time.

Caine watched with a smirk that spread across his face. Now the blade would truly come to life and feed off of Alistair. Making it stronger for when its true owner reveals himself. Alistair opened his eyes and took in a long relaxed breath of air.

"How do you feel?" Caine asked.

"Like taking on the world," replied Alistair with a dark and evil smile.

"Where do we start?"

"Perhaps King Aidan?"

"No worries, he has already been dealt with."

"Looks like it will be Briyodia."

"I thought they had a treaty with us?"

"They had a treaty with King Edward not with us."

"Are you sure about this?"

"Do you question me?"

"Not at all my King," Caine bowed. "I shall get the men ready for battle. Just one question?"

"What?"

"Will the Dark Knights be accompanying us?"

"They do thirst for blood."

"Give them the command as well as us and we shall obey," Caine bowed again.

"Caine?"

"Yes?"

"Kill the King and Queen, they are not needed."

"Yes my Lord."

Caine went and readied his men for war, some questioned why the Dark Ones were traveling with them. With others seeing it as a way to keep casualties for them to a minimum. The First Knight was quick to remind the men who were in charge. And if they didn't like it they could speak with King Alistair. The groans and moans stifled as going against the King would get you executed or thrown into the dungeons.

It was a four day ride to Briyodia, though for most men it would have taken a week. But the Black Knights were no mere men, they were not natural. And did not eat or sleep, which made keeping up with them very difficult. Once there Cain didn't make a plan of attack or for any such measures for a counter attack either.

Not many would expect a full on attack from a Kingdom that has signed a peace treaty. Caine didn't care who would die or survive, this was going according to his plans in the long run. If this didn't get Stilfadr's blood boiling and wanting a fight nothing would. Especially when he learns the King and Queen were murdered for no reason.

Caine felt no need to participate in the battle. He would sit back and watch the violence unfold. It would be unwise to get himself injured, or worse killed in a needless battle. When the time was right he would head inside the castle and carry out the dirty deed entrusted to him.

The battle was fierce, the knights of Briyodia fought valiantly against the enemy. But not even the most skilled was a match against the Dark Knights. They cut down any and all that stood in their way with little to no effort. Unfortunately even some of the Knight's Of Todrain were killed on the battlefield. The Dark Ones didn't have feelings nor cared who died, they just obeyed their one true master.

Screams echoed down the streets as the battle waged on, the townspeople were even killed by accident. Blood colored the streets a crimson red and flowed like an ocean. Caine smiled, a few less people in a kingdom that was being taken over never hurt anything. He was happy with what he had seen, this battle will be won in a matter of hours.

Which would mean they would be moving the King and Queen to a safe place. Probably means they would be taken to the stables and escape on horseback. Most Kings would stay until the very end protecting the people and his castle. But something told Caine that wouldn't be the case in this situation.

Caine went with his gut and instead of going inside the castle he made his way to the stables. And that is where he found them trying to escape, with what he believed was their best warriors protecting them. He unsheathed his blade ready for them to attack. But the King did not wish for a fight, instead he wanted a peaceful resolution.

"Why do you attack us?" The King questioned. "We have done nothing to break the treaty."

"King Alistair decided the treaty means nothing."

"Drasal has become home to the bloodthirsty."

"Says the great king that is leaving his people to die," Caine laughed.

"Making sure that I may rebuild my kingdom."

"Too bad you won't get the chance."

"One man can't stand up to three trained warriors."

Caine lifted his hand and motioned for them to bring the fight to him, "Let's see what you've got," he said.

The knights looked to their king for permission to attack. He gave the nod and they drew their weapons. It wasn't much of a fight as what most don't know is that Caine's blade can pierce ninety percent of all armor. He sidestepped one of the knights trying to slash at him. He brought his blade upward cutting through the backplate of his armor and into his flesh. Caine thrust the blade of his sword backwards killing the warrior behind him before he could finish his attack.

Caine then swung around and cut the last of the knights right leg off clean from the bone. Causing him to stumble over and fall into a puddle of his own blood. Caine stood straight up and wiped the blood from the blade. He slowly started to walk towards the King and Queen all that was heard was the sound of their screams coming from the stable.

The First Knight walked out right in the center of the town where the battle waged. He lifted the severed heads of the King and Queen of Briyodia. "Your King and Queen are dead!" He shouted. "There is no reason to continue the needless bloodshed! Kneel down and place your weapons on the ground and swear allegiance to King Alistair and we shall spare your lives.

The remaining knights did as asked and the war had ended. The Knights Of Valor celebrated and cheered for the day was won. Caine threw the heads on the ground and demanded they be placed on stakes for a warning to any that would oppose them. The Kingdom Of Briyodia now belonged to King Alistair.

Caine gave orders that his knights stay behind and implement the new laws. He would send a messenger when the time to return home was near. Anyone that would oppose them would suffer the same fate as the previous King and Queen. The First Knight returned home with news of their success.

Hearing the news brought a smile to Alistair's face. But his plans were not complete. There were other kingdoms that needed to learn the same lesson. The time had come to conquer an even stronger kingdom to send a message. And the message was that he was ready to reign over the new world order and he was one of the new gods to rule over all.

Next on the list was the kingdom of Pholum. Next to Todrain they were one of the strongest Kingdom's he would have to wage war against. Caine explained that most of the Knights had been held up at Briyodia. Alistair had no plans on storming through the front gates. Instead he was going to use the poison the Chamberlain had made from the plants he had acquired.

Alistair was going to have Caine release the poison in their water supply. Then plant the seeds of deception against the neighboring kingdom of Atricia. If all goes well they would rage war against one another and Drasal can swoop in and conquer another kingdom. Caine liked the idea but wanted to take it a step further.

He suggested that the poison be used on both the kingdoms water supply. If both kingdoms were taking care of the sick and the knights were too busy fighting one another it would be easy pickins. Caine could take his troops and the black knights and conquer both kingdoms one after another.

Alistair seemed to enjoy that idea even more, he just had one request. That he gets to lead the charge, the king wanted to see the carnage for himself. Also see if the poison was as potent as the Chamberlain claimed it would be. Caine was ecstatic that the king decided to come along, that would work in his favor. It was time to send a messenger to Stilfadr.

Stilfadr was out training when a man on a white and brown horse rode up. He showed no interest in the man and kept training with a hatchet in one hand and a shortsword in the other. His moves were swift and precise and he moved with a quickness that was surprising for a big man. Eventually he grew tired of being watched, "Is there something I can help you with?" He grumbled.

"Are you Stilfadr?" The rider asked.

"Who wants to know?"

"Shawn would like a message delivered to a man of that name. I was told I could find him out here."

"You don't look like a Knight."

"I'm not even a warrior, I was paid to deliver a message that is all."

"Then yes I am the man you seek."

The rider handed over a rolled up piece of parchment paper, "The job is done. I wish you well sir," he said before pulling the reins of the horse and riding away.

Stilfadr unrolled the paper and began reading what had been written. It was a message from Shawn like the rider had stated. He wanted Stilfadr and few of his men to visit the Kingdom Of Pholum in a weeks time. It stated that Shawn had something urgent he needed to show him. Still he didn't know what to think. Trust was a big thing, if you trusted the wrong person it ended badly.

And Shawn was a man of mystery, he didn't look to be much of a fighter. But the way he carried himself told Stilfadr a differently. Shawn was no slouch nor just some ordinary man, plus he stole from a castle which is no easy feat. Also, who were these people that Shawn claimed he was working with.

Stilfadr had a tough choice to make. Trust in Shawn and go to Pholum and walk into a possible trap. Or stay away and miss what could be something that sway the fates in his direction. He took this message back to his hideout wanting to talk it over with his men.

They were not trusting in the message delivered to their leader. Most viewed this as a trap and believed if they went to the kingdom suggested it would lead to an ambush. Stilfadr was a great leader and people were drawn to him. Even if they didn't know him warriors would follow him into battle.

And King's like Alistair would want him dead instead of having him fighting on the battlefield. Though if their leader wished it they would follow him into the flames of Hades. His men's opinions meant a lot to him as a leader. But he had to go with his gut feeling, something deep down pulled him towards Pholum. So he gathered three of his best fighters though they grumbled about his choice. By the time they made it to Pholum it had been a weeks time like the message stated.

It took them by surprise by what they had seen upon their arrival. People were being slaughtered on the streets, their corpses were thrown on top of one another and set a blaze. It was heartbreaking to witness, it didn't matter if it were a woman or child they were being killed. And there wasn't anything Stilfadr or his men could do about it.

For a brief moment he pondered on where the King or Queen could be. And why nothing was being done to save the people of Pholum. Then it became clear to them why nothing was done to help. The good King and Queen were dead, their heads placed on stakes for the world to see. Which leads to the question. Why the needless bloodshed?

Upon closer look at the colors of the flag the attacking Knights bore was telling. It was the Knights of Valor and by the looks of things this fight was over. Stilfadr had heard legends about the Knights Of Valor, they protected the weak, gave people hope in the darkest of times. You had to train endlessly just to be considered to become one of their ranks.

He had even heard stories about the now, King Alistair. He fought and clawed from a very young age to become a Knight Of Valor. With his grit and tenacity he caught the eye of King Edward and quickly became the youngest First Knight in history. Unfortunately Alistair started to dabble in the Dark Arts. This started his descent into madness, and he eventually killed Edward and took the crown for himself.

Though this is just hearsay and if you hear others talk. They state that King Edward was weak and feeble. Rarely was he spotted out of the castle, and when he was seen he never looked healthy. This caused concern from the people that their King may no longer be able to protect them. One day Edward just vanished, never to be heard from again.

If you ask the people most of them will tell you Alistair has been a great king. Kind, generous, just in his cause to bring all Kingdoms under one banner of peace. Looking at this pointless battle along with murdering most of the townspeople. It would seem Alistair's so called one kingdom of peace is one big load of bullshit.

Stilfadr now realized if the King's ambition of a one world kingdom came to fruition. It would be ruled with an iron fist, terrorizing the weak for pleasure. Using fear as a weapon of choice would be front and center as it is now. It was evident that something had to be done, Alistair had to be stopped at all cost. Or a darkness unlike any other would plague the lands once more.

Caine stood off in the shadows using magic to keep himself out of Stilfadr's sight. The look on the barbarians face was priceless, his plan was now set in motion. Soon he would have the man eating right out of his hands, willing to do whatever was suggested. Once the news spread that Alistair and the Dark Knights were seen burning Atricia to the ground. Caine would have many more fools wanting to join the witch hunt.

Within a handful weeks the Kingdom Of Drasal had conquered many. This had made Caine of better spirit as well the same for Alistair. Both men were quite happy that their agendas were closing in on fruition. Caine had heard great news of Ulrich's progression training with Zerius. While Alistair was overjoyed to hear this as well not realizing it would be his downfall in the months to come.

Alistair had sent word to Caine that he was needed in the king's chambers. It was time for them to discuss their next move and Alistair had the perfect target yet again. He was ready to take the fight to the Elves and show the true power he possessed.

"I must change your mind about this," Caine insisted. "This is not a wise decision at this time."

"Are you afraid of them?" Alistair laughed. "Even though I hold the blade of legend."

"It's not that my Lord."

"Then what?"

"The Elves are powerful and their Elder is strong in the ways of earth magic."

"What are you getting at?"

"In your state she may be able to break your connection with the blade. If the Dark Ones turned against us at such a time we would lose everything we've accomplished thus far," Caine explained.

"Are you suggesting that I am weak?" Alistair hissed.

"To be honest, yes you're clearly weakened from the last couple of battles," Caine responded. "Controlling the Dark Knights has taken a toll on your body and mind."

"But I feel fine," Alistair retorted.

"Take a look at the blade," Caine insisted.

Alistair stood and unsheathed the cursed sword, something about it was off. The power he used to feel radiating from blade seemed lesser than normal. Also the color seemed dull, not the bright purple he had grown accustomed to over the past couple of years. "What has happened?"

"Your body and mind has weakened," said Caine. "Rest is what is needed. Once you awaken you will know the time is right to take on the Elves."

"Good," Alistair smiled. "I shall head for my sleeping quarters and do as asked of me. Be prepared when I wake up for we go to battle once more."

"One question before you go."

"Speak what is on your mind."

"Why do you wish to go to war with such a powerful enemy?"

"The Elves I am after helped the ones who would stand against us get away."

"I see," Caine said. "We do need to act upon such arrogance. Send a message to others that helping the enemy will not be tolerated."

"I knew you would see things my way." Alistair turned and walked away leaving Caine to his own devices.

Caine knew the Alistair's body and mind was drained. Not that he cared but he did need Alistair somewhat sane to complete his agenda. However, he did not expect the king to sleep for almost two weeks. That put some strain on trying to meet with Stilfadr in just a week's time. On top of that Alistair was intent on waging war with the Elves right then and there.

"Give me time to gather my knights," Caine insisted.

"This time it will be just me and you along with the Dark Ones," Alistair responded.

"Our men need to be seen in battle my Lord."

"Not this time."

"But it is good for morale."

"I don't want the Knights Of Valor to take part in this."

"That makes no sense."

"Caine you know as well as I do the Elves are all about peace and nature. I agree that some of the Knights would follow us into any battle. But others may start a revolt after seeing what I am about to do. I would like to avoid such a headache."

It would seem Alistair hadn't lost his mind to the blade afterall, Caine thought to himself. Though he was right, it would be unwise for a revolt in the ranks to begin now when he was so close. Yet he was still nervous about facing off against Allora and her Elven warriors. They may believe in peace but they will still fight to protect themselves and their home. If Alistair weakens further he will lose control over the blade and the Dark Knights.

But that possibility mattered not to Alistair, he was awake and craving bloodshed. Which meant the blade was hungry for more souls to take. Nothing was going to calm that urge and it was time to let the time bomb explode. It's target was the Elves hiding away in Hyss Woods. Allora was going to be a formattable opponent though it was too late to turn back now.

Allora must have known they were coming as she cast a spell of protection over the woods and Rehakadi. Allowing a very strong electrical mist to surround the woods. Not even the Dark Ones could break through the mist. It was going to take some powerful magic to break through the barrier in place.

"Looks like it will be up to me," said Alistair with a sword already in hand.

"You will have to give a lot of yourself to the blade and it may not even work," warned Caine.

"It will work," Alistair replied. "Don't worry about me, I know what my body and mind can handle."

Caine stepped aside, "If that is what you wish," he bowed.

Alistair closed his eyes and focused his anger and rage towards Allora and her subjects. At first it didn't seem to work, was his strength starting to diminish? Or did he have to give something more? He couldn't give anymore of his mind or his body. What else could he give, there had to be something.

Then it dawned upon him what the blade wanted. Zerius warned him that this day would come. A day where he would have to give the ultimate sacrifice in order to keep this power. The cursed sword wanted his soul or he would lose the power to create his own world. But he was a god and people needed to learn that.

So he made the decision to give into what it wanted. Alistair connected with the blade and promised to give up his soul. That's when he heard a voice inside his head. It was something that had never happened until now, until he decided to give in.

The voice was dark and menacing when it spoke to him, "Someone other than the chosen has control over the blade? Impressive."

"I have complete control over you," Alistair bolstered.

"You have control over the blade not me," the voice stated. "Must be losing your strength. Am I right?"

"My strength but not my mind."

"Again, impressive. And you wish to give your soul to the blade?"

"I do."

"Do you understand what that means?"

"The blade gets my soul and I get ultimate power."

"Be warned that whatever feelings you once had will no longer exist."

"That will be a blessing."

"One more thing you must know."

"What is that?"

"You will share your body with me when the time comes."

"It is a burden I am willing to accept."

"Then we have a deal?"

"Yes we have a deal." A dark aura surrounded Alistair's body, and the last thing he heard was a sinister laugh. The cursed blade erupted with power and easily pierced through the protective barrier. Causing the mist to slowly disappear. "Too easy." He smiled and sounded as evil as ever.

"Lord Alistair?" He turned and looked at Caine with eyes

glowing a dark purple almost black coloration. His facial expressions had changed to a point where he no longer looked human. "You're not Alistair are you?" He questioned.

"Whatever do you mean?"

"I am no fool," said Caine. "I've known Alistair for years and you are not him."

"Perhaps this will answer your question." He turned to the Dark Knights and announced their leader had returned. Every one of them kneeled and bowed bowed before him. This time it didn't seem forced like the other time he announced his control over them.

"So Alistair finally gave himself over to the blade," Caine laughed.

"And his body and soul now belong to me."

"The Dark Lord graces us with his presence."

"In the flesh."

"Though that flesh won't last long nor will the mind."

"It will last long enough until I find the one."

"What about the Elves?"

"I have to keep up appearances and I hate the Elven people and long to destroy them."

"What shall we do my King?" Caine bowed hiding the smile on his face.

"Kill everyone and burn the woods to ground."

"As you wish."

CHAPTER THIRTEEN

TIME TO LEARN THE TRUTH

Captain Bosch had done what was asked of him he had gotten them to the Isle Hesta where the Tomb Of Carnage is said to preside. They didn't need the Captain anymore. Supposedly, the tomb could teleport the ones that survive anywhere their hearts desire. The need for a ship helping their travels had come to an end. It was time for the Captain's fate to be decided.

Gawain and Aurelius wanted to spill Bosch's blood, but Leon reminded them of the promise they had made. And he didn't want to be like Alistair and Caine. Nor did he want Aurelius or Gawain to walk the path of darkness either. Even though he sold them out bloodshed wasn't the answer.

"He doesn't deserve to live!" Gawain argued.

"Agreed," said Aurelius.

"I upheld my end of the deal." Bosch pointed out that fact rather quickly.

"Though you have yet to be punished for betraying us," replied Aurelius. "If you did it once, what's to stop you from doing it again?"

"If not for me you wouldn't have come this far," Bosch responded back.

"I've heard enough of this." Gawain unsheathed his blade ready to take his revenge. Leladda acted and put herself in Gawain's direct path, "Move out of my way," he hissed.

"Don't forget who you work for," she said. "Killing him is not part of your mission. Leon has wished for that bastard to be spared and I'm sure he has a reason. Put that sword away and let's go find my father."

"Please do as she says," begged Cathrine.

"Fine," Gawain grunted and sheathed his blade back to his side.

"I don't work for you and Bosch must pay some kind of penance for his crime," Aurelius said.

"Leave him be," Leon replied. "It's not worth it."

"Even after what he has done to us? He tortured us for almost a year, and was going to take us to Alistair for even more gold. Didn't care if we lived or died or who he had to hurt," Aurelius explained.

"His blood will only taint this holy ground. Is that something you want?" Leon responded.

Aurelius didn't think about what could happen if tainted blood such as the Captain's touched the ground of such a place. It could curse the rest of their journey and change their fortunes. Instead of killing Bosch he made a promise. That when the journey ended he would find Bosch, even if it meant going to the ends of the earth. That's when he would take his revenge.

Bosch smiled, "It's been interesting to say the least. Aurelius I hope you stay alive long enough to hunt me down. May your travels end well." He bowed and walked away as quickly as one possibly could without running.

"Hope you know what you're doing," Gawain said.

"He's no longer a concern," Leon replied.

"Finding my father is," said Leladda.

"And finding the entrance to the tomb," Leon added.

"Which way from here?" Aurelius asked.

"I will lead the way to the tomb," Cathrine interrupted.

"How will you be able to do that?" Leon questioned.

"The light of the goddess will guide us there," she answered.

"I don't see anything," Leon said scratching his head.

"Only she can see it," Gawain responded.

"Can you see anything?" Leon looked at Aurelius and asked.

"No," he said. "But I can sense something beyond our comprehension waits for us here."

"Is my father here?" Leladda asked.

"There is life here, some humans and something darker," Aurelius replied.

"It has to be your father," said Cathrine. "Because the energy here is almost the same as yours."

"Do you know where he's at?"

"His energy is faint. I would guess he is already inside the tomb ahead of us."

"We must hurry!" Leladda exclaimed. "He could be in danger."

"Form a circle around me," Cathrine said. "Protect me from all that may come. My being here will stir up some restless spirits wishing for me to take them to the afterlife."

They walked on ahead with Cathrine in the center, Gawain led in the front. While Aurelius and Leon stood to the left and right of her, while Leladda brought up the back. Leon was keeping a close eye out for anything and everything. Though this island didn't feel like holy ground as the dragon had claimed it to be.

It felt a little dark to him and the air seemed filled with sorrow. The ground looked chard and he didn't see any vegetation. There was a resemblance of what may have once been trees but that was all. He couldn't see any wildlife or any other signs of life for that matter. But something out of the corner of his eye caught his attention.

There was an old church of light off to his left, it was beaten and battered but still stood. Something about it seemed all too familiar, he tried but he couldn't put his finger on it. Little did he know that he was standing still staring off in that direction. Cathrine was the first to notice Leon wasn't with the group. When she looked back she could see him a ways back just standing there.

"Wait," Cathrine demanded.

"What is it?" Gawain asked.

"Something is wrong with Leon."

"Where is he?" Aurelius questioned.

"I didn't even notice he was gone," Leladda said.

"He's back there looking at something," Cathrine said.

"I will go get him," said Leladda before taking off after him.

"Shouldn't we go after her?" Cathrine asked.

"Wouldn't do us any good," Gawain replied.

"He's right," Aurelius chuckled.

Leladda was going to run up to Leon but was afraid she would startle him. She decided it would be best to slow her pace and approach him cautiously. Leon didn't seem like he was in a daze or a trance like state. Though he did look as if he was trying to sort out his thoughts. Perhaps whatever he was looking at was familiar in some way.

"Leon?"

He turned to look at her, "Do you see that over there?"

"Looks like an old church," she replied. "What about it?"

"So you see it?"

"Yes, I do." She looked confused. "Why?"

"I've seen it before."

"Where?"

"In a dream or another world it's hard to explain."

"Is it that important?"

"Possibly."

Leladda smirked, "Let's go check it out."

"That will put us behind," Leon responded.

"Could be something important inside waiting for you. Sure you want to pass that up?"

"After you," Leon smiled.

"You're the one with the powers not me," Leladda laughed. "How about we do this together."

Leon and Leladda walked towards the church together, the closer they got the more ran down it was looking. However it still stood in one piece, and the double doors blocking entrance was still there as well. Inside everything started to come back to him bit by bit. Leon mumbled a few words under his breath and the torches in the room began to catch fire.

"How did you do that?" Leladda asked.

Leon ignored her question and walked on ahead, until he came upon the statue of the goddess Celestial. "This can't be," he muttered. He fumbled around until he found what felt like a switch and flipped it. The statue started to tremble before moving off to the side, revealing a passageway.

"This is starting to worry me," Leladda said.

"That makes two of us." Leon walked further on ahead with Leladda following in pursuit. If his assumption was correct they would exit into some type of training grounds. At the end of the tunnel he let out a gasp of disbelief as did she.

"What is this place?" Leladda gasped.

"The training grounds."

"Why does it look different than the rest of the land?"

"It was untouched by the war."

"What war?"

Leon walked around touching everything in his path, he even picked up the wooden swords Robin made him train with. He smiled and took a couple of swings with it before tossing it to the side. Leon made his way over to where a bow and arrow stood next to a wooden fence. There was a target about forty feet ahead of him. There were two arrows stuck in the target.

To his bewilderment it was the same two arrows that he and Robin shot into the target. He bent over and picked up the bow and arrow, placing the arrow on the bow, he pulled the string back and aimed at the target. He let go of the string and the arrow zipped through the air splitting the arrow in the target in half.

"Lucky shot." For a second he thought he heard Robin's voice, when he turned it was Leladda standing there not Robin. "You look shocked. Was it something I said?"

Leon shook his head, "For a second I thought you were someone else."

"A ghost from the past?" She asked. "Have you figured out where we are?"

He nodded, " I have," Leon replied.

"And?" A voice from afar questioned, when they turned around the rest of the group had joined them.

"What is this place?" Aurelius asked.

"Training grounds," Gawain answered in Leon's place.

"How did you know?" replied Leon.

"I know training grounds when I see them. Why did you two run off?"

"I was chasing after him," said Leladda.

"My fault," Leon added.

"Do you know where we find ourselves, Leon?" Cathrine questioned.

"At first things seemed familiar to me," Leon answered. "When we walked inside the church it became clear to me. This is where I would travel too after touching pieces of that cursed blade. Where a man named Robin trained me, explained to me about my bloodline. Though it didn't look this way when I came here. This is where the Great War took place."

"Is he right?" Gawain looked at Cathrine and asked.

"He is. This is the main battlefield for the Great War. Where the four brave heroes with help from the other races and the Dragons defeated the Dark Lord and sealing away his soul inside his very own creation, the Reaper blade."

"I never heard of this," said Gawain.

"The Academy never taught the full story," Cathrine responded.

"Why would it be kept from us?"

"King Edward didn't want the full truth to be told."

"Then how do you know the full truth?"

“I wasn’t always with the Academy, you know this Gawain. The church of light taught me the real truth.”

“That’s not the whole truth,” Leon informed her. “I know a little more than that, but will learn the full truth inside the tomb. Especially the truth about me.”

“We can discuss this later,” Gawian interrupted. “Remember we have to be at the tomb when the moonlight fills the night sky.”

“Before we go I must give a warning. Leladda’s father and his men will be waiting for us. We will surely be walking into a trap for they can’t gain entrance into the tomb with this amulet. Trust me when I say they are not inside like you think,” explained Leon.

“I will handle my father,” Leladda responded.

The sun was starting to set an eerie feeling of being followed was falling over the group as they were getting closer to the tomb. Either it was human or spirit something was indeed in pursuit. Could be because of Cathrine being a follower of the light. Though it was more likely that the chosen one was there instead.

But it wasn’t Leladda’s father or he would have made his move by now. Cathrine warned that they were getting closer to the tomb and the energy she was sensing was getting stronger. Leladda pleaded with them not to draw their weapons. Blood being spilled was pointless, she was sure she could get through to him.

“Do not take another step,” a voice warned. “Now turn around slowly.” When they turned around Leladda was quickly recognized. “Princess Leladda,” the knight gasped as he sheathed his blade. “What are you doing here?”

“Looking for my father,” she answered.

“King Thomas would not be happy to see you here.”

Leladda looked around, “Where is my father? Is he not with you?”

The knight lowered his head, “He was approached by some spirit or something not sure what it was to be honest. It spoke in some strange tongue, but your father seemed to understand what it was saying. He then asked for a few men to stand by them and just like that they vanished into thin air."

"You let him go!" Leladda shouted.

"I had no choice, he's the King."

"Is there another way into the tomb?" Gawain assumed.

"It would make sense a spirit would know of another way," Cathrine agreed. "But it would want something in return."

"Looks like we are about to find out," Leon interrupted. "The moon is about to show us the way." He took the amulet from around his neck, "I hope you're right about this Robin," Leon muttered. He held up the relic and the rays of light from the moon shined through the center of the amulet.

The focused light from the amulet shone upon the ground and the earth began to tremble. The ground parted and a large stone pillar started to rise from the earth. Revealing steps forming one by one leading down below the earth's crust. A red glow emanated from below, the heat rising proved that it must have been lava.

"I hate tombs," Gawain muttered under his breath. "Especially this one."

"Only three of us can enter from here," Leon told them.

"I'm going," Leladda stuberingly said.

"That leaves one more," said Leon. "Who's it going to be?"

"Can we all not go?" Aurelius asked.

Leon shook his head, "Only three may enter," he said again. "More will only anger the God that looks over this place."

"He knows he will have better odds if the numbers are less," Gawain grumbled.

"Why all the talk? Let's get moving," Leladda demanded.

"I have to lead the way," Leon said. "One more thing, be on guard, who knows what we may cross paths with down there." Leon took a few steps down into the depths of the tomb. The closer they got to the bottom he felt like something or someone was expecting him. Knew he would be there on this night of all nights.

He had to push that thought to the back of his mind, if he was distracted it could be their end. His thoughts had to be clear of any doubt or feelings of fear. He was here and there was no turning back, even though a nagging voice was telling him to do so.

Leon was struggling to remember the way, then it hit him, he didn't know anything about this place. But then something Robin told him resurfaced in his thoughts. Inside the tomb ask for help where you believe there is none. The chosen shall be pointed the way if his heart is brave. Robin didn't say anything about asking aloud, Leon thought to himself.

Leon pointed straight ahead and focused his mind on connecting with whatever dwelled in this place. I am the chosen you have been waiting for, though I don't know the way. Please I beg that you guide my feet so that I may find you. He repeated that saying over and over in his mind hoping that it was not in vain. When he opened his eyes his finger was pointing in a different direction Gawain and Leladda were heading in.

"Where are you guys going?" Leon quietly asked. "That's not the way."

"Why are you speaking so softly?" Leladda asked.

"Best not to be heard," Gawain answered in Leon's place. "Are you sure that's the way."

Leon nodded and motioned for them to follow his lead. Just like all the times before Gawain learned it was pointless to argue with him. Another fifty minutes into the tomb felt more like three weeks. Being surrounded by lava was starting to make it feel like they were heading deeper into the underworld.

After much walking thinking Leon was guiding them in the right direction the small group happened upon a dead end. Both Gawain and Leladda voiced their frustrations. Leon had to work hard to convince them this was the path they must take.

"Are you sure about this?" Gawain asked.

"This is the right way!" Leon exclaimed.

"I say we turn back," Leladda hissed.

"You can't," Leon replied.

"Why can't we?"

"The way back has been blocked," Leon sighed.

"What!" She exclaimed. "We're stuck here?"

"This is the way, I just have to figure it out!" Leon shouted back.

"Calm yourselves!" Gawain demanded. "This is exactly what he wants."

"Who wants?"

"The so called god of this cave. He doesn't want us to survive, trust me, I know how he works. Focus on finding a way through before the heat from the lava burns the flesh from our bones."

Leon took a few deep breaths to calm himself even though it felt like fire on his lungs it did the trick. He took a knife from his belt and wrapped his hand around the sharp blade. Pulling down on the hilt the blade cut into the palm of his hand.

"Do you think it will work like last time?" asked Gawain.

Leon shrugged, "One way to find out." He smeared his own blood on the stonewall in front of them. An outline of a door appeared before them along with the same ancient language they had seen before. "Looks like it worked," he smirked. "Will you read it for us Gawain?"

"Hmm." Gawain rubbed his chin as he took a closer look at the writing, "This one is more complicated than the last time," he said. "It's a riddle we must solve to open the door. I crawl when I am young, walk when I am older, then find myself crawling once more."

"What in the hell does that mean?" Leladda grumbled.

"It's man," Leon responded. "That's the answer."

"Then why does the door not open?" Gawain asked. "Must be something else."

"Wait, wait, wait. Can you speak the language? Not just read it?"

"I'm a little rusty, but I can try," Gawain responded. "I believe the word for man is tiam." Leon was right, when man was spoken in the ancient tongue the stone door opened. They did wonder what was on the other side waiting in the darkness for them. The answer would come sooner than later as Leladda pushed them ahead.

Gawain knew of things that were in this tomb, the self proclaimed god of this tomb was just a portion of what dwelled here. Any kind of loud noises and those blasted Umbramen would come running. What he wasn't thinking of was their sent was no longer hidden. And could already smell their flesh and blood inside the tomb.

A thunderous noise filled the tomb that caught the group by surprise. It was clear to them what it was, that was the sound of weapons being drummed against shields. A warning that the enemy was coming for them and a fight for survival was about to begin.

"Umbramen," Gawain spate. "Thought for sure we had been quite enough."

"They picked up on our scent," said Leon.

"Damn, I forgot about that."

"Shouldn't we be getting the hell out of here?" Leladda replied.

"Right," Gawain agreed. "We may have to cut our way through no matter what happens keep moving."

Gawain couldn't have been more correct. Those smelly bastards had them surrounded. The only way to get through was to fight, it was the only choice given. They should count their lucky stars the Umbramen don't use bow and arrows. Their weapons of choice are strictly hatchets and sharpened ended shields.

Choosing the right path while fighting was easier said than done. When you have three different paths, one to the left, one to the right, and straight ahead, the chosen path had to be the right one. Leon was the only one able to lead the way. The others couldn't see the right path to take like he could.

As Leon fought on, he heard a voice in his head telling him to take the path to the left. He announced that to the others, unfortunately that way seemed to be where most of the Umbramen were coming from. Gawain was using his new fighting techniques he had learned. He used his sword to cut the legs out from one enemy and the hatchet he carried to split the skull of another.

Leladda was no slouch with the blade for someone who had been locked away in a castle for that long of time. She fought with a tenacity that reminded both men of Ellyn in a way though not as skilled. Leon had what he felt as a strange urge to protect her. Watching her have to fight made him somewhat angry.

Leon dropped his guard for a brief moment and in a blink of an eye he found himself surrounded on an island all alone. He wasn't afraid, his skill was above and beyond what it once was. Leon stabbed one through the face with his blade. Took up the hatchet and lopped off the head of another. Then threw the small axe at the Umbramen that was sprinting towards him. The hatchet flew through the air hitting its target right between the eyes.

While that was going on Leladda had been taken to ground. Leon feared the worst had happened and his powers erupted. He rushed through three of the Umbramen like they were nothing. He swung his sword and a blue light flashed knocking the group of Umbramen back killing most of them. Leon reached down lifted Leladda to her feet and told her to run.

Gawain and Leladda made it through and to the path safely. Leon knew these creatures would not give up. Something had to be done to ensure they wouldn't be followed. He had an idea it was time to test the sword, Leon forced the blade into the ground. Causing an explosion that brought that part of the tomb to come trembling down on top of the Umbramen.

Leon was impressed, even without it being restored the blade was powerful. He gave a sigh of relief when he found out that Leladda was unharmed. They were just happy to rid themselves of the Umbramen.

"I hope my father got past those things," Leladda said with a look of worry on her face.

"I'm sure he's fine," Leon responded. "Let's keep going."

"Wait," Gawain said.

"What?" Leon responded. "We need to hurry on our way."

"I need to tell you what you will face from here."

"I already know."

Gawain shook his head, "No you don't," he insisted. "What you believe is the god of this tomb. Is actually a spirit called Hollowsword, he's the protector of this place."

"Have you been here before?" Leon questioned.

"I have," he answered.

Leon's brow raised, "How is that possible?"

"It was one of my first missions for the Academy. The Master at the time wanted something from inside the tomb. To be honest it was the same artifact that your father is after, Leladda."

"So you knew where he was going the whole time?!" She snapped.

"I did."

"Why didn't we come here first?"

"I was hoping we could catch him before he came this far. To talk him out of this fool's errand before it was too late."

"What are you not telling us?" Leon questioned. "And how in the hell did you get inside?"

"Hollowsword has a what you would call a pet. It will get you inside without the amulet if you feed it human flesh." Gawain sighed, "The relic your father seeks will consume his life in order for him to communicate with the dead."

"What else is there?" Leon hissed.

"Don't worry about that we have to stop my father!" Leladda shouted before running on ahead. With Gawain and Leon given chase trying to stop her from doing something stupid. Then out of the blue she just vanished into thin air.

"Leladda!" They both shouted over and over again to no avail.

"Where did she go?" Leon shouted.

"Where her heart desires," said a voice.

"Who's there? Show yourself!" Leon demanded.

A man stepped from the shadows and into the light. He was a beast of a man, tall and muscular. Bore a silver plated armor and carried a large two handed bastard sword. His helmet did completely cover his face and overly large beard. His eyes burned with the strength of a thousand men. "You made it this far on your own. Am I right to presume you're the chosen one?" He asked.

"And if I'm not?" Leon retorted.

"Then I will have to feed you to my pet. Though I already knew who you were. I assume you are here about that blade you carry?"

"I need to bring it back to life," Leon replied. "And you're going to tell me how."

"I like how the fire burns inside of you," Hollowsword laughed. "Allow me to explain how this works. You will do battle with me, if you win then I will restore the blade to its former glory."

"And if I lose?"

"You die and that power of yours becomes mine to do with as I please."

Leon glanced over at Gawain, "You knew about this didn't you?" He asked.

"Why do you think I didn't want us to come here?"

"You didn't believe I was yet ready for this did you?"

"No," Gawain replied. "And I didn't want to see you die after I made a promise to keep you safe."

"Enough talk!" Hollowsword belted. "Step up and face me chosen one."

Leon stepped forward and unsheathed his blade, "Just keep your promise when I defeat you," he said.

"Shame I have to kill you. I really do like your spirit."

"It won't be as easy as you think," smiled Leon. He lifted his blade and readied himself for an attack. Hollowsword disappeared and reappeared behind Leon. The young man spun around and blocked the oncoming attack. "Is that the best you've got?" Leon responded still with that smile on his face.

Leon tapped into the power that dwells deep within like Robin had trained him to do. He used that power to knock Hollowsword back and dashed forward with an attack of his own. Though the spirit warrior easily parried and countered. Leon was able to parry the counter attack, both warriors seemed very pleased with themselves.

"Practice time is over," said Leon.

"Agreed," Hollowsword replied.

Both readied themselves and dashed forward with blinding speed. Gawain stood off to the side watching barely able to keep up with their movements. He could feel immense power radiating each time their blades connected with one another. Gawain prayed to the gods that Leon would come out the victor. For that young man would be the only one that could help stop Alistair and Caine.

"As much fun as this has been it's time to end this," Hollowsword proclaimed. The warrior swung his blade with intentions of destroying Leon's blade and killing the young man using it. At the last second Leon held up his hand catching the blade with ease. "How did you do that?" Hollowsword gasped.

"You look surprised," Leon said. "Yes, I caught your blade. Is that such a mind blowing thing to you?" Hollowsword pulled back and retreated a few steps. "Why do you retreat? Such a strange reaction for a god."

"Do not speak as though you've won this battle," Hollowsword spate. "This is far from over."

"Really?" Leon smirked. "Your power is fading, I would say this fight is at its end."

"Then I will use the power of the gods to finish this!" Hollowsword's body bulked up ten fold. His sword beamed with a bright red light, to Leon it felt like the spirit would explode from such power. Again Hollowsword darted forward with great intensity and speed. Something in the pit of Leon's stomach told him he had to stand against this attack to truly be the victor.

Leon dropped his guard accepting the oncoming attack. When Hollowsword's blade made contact an explosion filled the tomb. With enough force that sent Gawain hurlying backwards and onto the ground. He slowly got to his feet fearing the worst for Leon. He began to frantically search the area.

There was a cloud of dust that made seeing extremely hard. Even though he could not see anything he still sensed life. He couldn't be sure if it was Leon or the spirit warrior that won the day. When the dust settled he could see both of them were still standing. "Thank the gods," Gawain muttered to himself.

"Looks like you're still standing," Hollowsword said. "And with little to no damage."

"Is the fight over?" Leon huffed.

"It is."

"Then tell me how to make the blade whole again."

"Hold the blade up and take a look."

Leon held up the sword, it was starting to take shape before his very eyes. The hilt was no longer a dark color, for it had changed to a bright gold. And the purple jewel that Mokgrith had replaced had turned into a clear crystal. The blade itself had changed as well, the dark coloration crumbled away showing a bright silver in its place. Is this truly the legendary blade Nightbane? He thought to himself.

"That truly is Nightbane's true form," Hollowsword said.

"How was it restored?" Leon questioned.

"When you accepted my attack without defending allowed the sword to recognize you as its true owner. That in itself brought the blade back to life."

"What would have happened if I blocked the attack?"

"Simple, you would have perished. The blade would have taken your life and I would have a new artifact for my tomb."

"I was also told I would learn the truth here."

"Would you accept it if I told you?"

"Try me."

"You truly are your father's son."

"What would you know of my father?"

"I fought with him on the battlefield."

"How is that possible?"

"I was one of the four. Your father and mother, Edward and myself. We were chosen to defeat the Dark Lord, though we couldn't do it with our strength alone. We took the power of the gods to aid us in the fight."

"And that's when the weapons were created?" Leon asked.

"Correct. We became heroes on that day and disposed of Cromwell and the Dark Ones."

"Yet your bloodline became cursed like mine."

"Your bloodline is not cursed. You have the blood of a hero flowing through your veins. Only one bloodline was cursed, and that was the Cromwell bloodline."

"My father was of that bloodline."

"Yet he became a great hero."

"Then explain the power that dwells within me. And why am I destined to destroy or save the world?"

"Your power came to be because your father's bloodline was chosen by the gods to save the world from the one that would destroy it. From the cursed one walking the path of darkness."

"There is another like me? Who is it?"

"You will find that out soon enough. Now I will help you exit this place after that my spirit can rest in peace. I wish you well chosen one. Close your eyes and focus on where you would like to be and who you would like to go with."

Leon closed his eyes and focused on his homeland as the place he would like to be. He also focused on Aurelius, Cathrine, Gawain, Leladda and her father and all the others. He felt a sensation of floating in the sky and the cool breeze hitting his face. Not much longer after that he felt the ground beneath his feet again. When Leon opened his eyes everyone one of his friends and the ones he didn't know were standing before him.

Leladda was slightly confused but grateful to be breathing in fresh once again. And was ecstatic to see her father on the outside with her, so much so she ran up and gave him a hug. King Thomas gave her a warm smile but you could see he was ashamed of his actions up to that point. He turned to look at the rag tag group before him. "You must be the ones that have been looking after my daughter," he said.

"More than I can say for you," Leon grunted.

Thomas lowered his head, “I deserve that.”

“Why did you put her through all this pain?” Gawain asked.

“I owe everyone here an explanation,” Thomas responded. “All I wanted was to see my wife again. When I heard about Hade’s Eye, I knew it was my only chance. It wasn’t long before I had lost my mind and perspective. If it wasn’t for Leladda showing up when she did, my life would have been taken by the Eye. Seems my kingdom needs me now more than ever,” Thomas sighed. “And so does the Queen, and Brolene needs to learn his place.”

“What will you do from here?” Leon asked Leladda.

“Head back home with my father,” she answered. “See that certain people get what's coming to them. And keep the promise we made to Mokgrith and bring him the hammer he requested. What about you?”

“It’s time I head back home,” Leon responded. “I have some unfinished business there.”

“I guess it’s time we go our separate ways,” Leladda said. She turned to Gawain and tossed a money bag over to him, “Thank you for all you’ve done, Gawain. As promised here’s the rest of the gold and silver owed to you.”

“Thank you, Leladda,” Gawain bowed. “It has been a pleasure, safe travels to you and yours.”

“Likewise,” Leladda smiled.

“Goodbye Leladda,” said Leon. “May our paths cross again someday.” Leladda gave Leon a kiss on the cheek before turning to walk away. Leon felt a warm fuzzy feeling building in the pit of his stomach. It was a feeling he had never felt before. Was this the same feelings that Ulrich had for Ellyn but stronger? No wonder he was so upset when he left the group that day.

“What are we going to do?” Cathrine asked Gawain.

“We head back home,” Gawain answered.

“Are you not going to help Leon?” She questioned.

“That’s up to him.”

“What do you have in mind?” Leon asked.

"Well we can't take on the Knights Of Valor and the Dark Knights without help can we?"

"I'm listening."

"I say we go and enlist some help. Pay Micha and King Peregrine a visit and hopefully get aid from the Knights Of Wespington. Afterwards we go and gather the rest of my men."

"What about the Elves?" Aurelius interrupted. "Don't forget I have soldiers of my own."

"You've done enough already old friend," Gawain responded. "I do not wish to drag you into this as well."

"I'm seeing this through to the end," Aurelius responded. "Like it or not."

"First Wespington, then gather the rest of Gawain's men, and then we pay a visit to Hyss Woods. Are we all in agreement?" Leon said. Both Aurelius and Gawain agreed that would be the best course of action. They had only hoped things would go according to plan. For the fight of their lives was near.

CHAPTER FOURTEEN

LIVES WILL CHANGE FOREVER

Ellyn was sitting in the throne room visiting with her brother and sister. When Shena walked into the room, followed by the Black Knight that aided them in rescuing Rin. Shena bowed, "Forgive me my lady for the interruption. Rowan wishes to speak with Ellyn and refuses to take no for an answer," she explained.

"That is up to my sister," Queen Mina responded. "What do you say Sis?"

"If not for Rowan none of us would be here right now," Ellyn said. "Of course I will speak with him."

"I would rather speak with you in private," Rowan insisted.

"Does The House Of Knowledge work?" Ellyn asked.

"Of course."

Ellyn led the way to The House Of Knowledge while Rown kept stride for stride with her. Once there Ellyn wished to know what Rowan wanted with her. He seemed somewhat nervous at first, but with a little more persistence he started to talk.

"So you want me to help you fight?" She asked.

"That is the sum of it."

"Just me?"

"And anyone else you can spare."

"Who are we fighting?"

"The King of Drasal."

"Alistair," she gasped. "Why ask me to do that?"

"Are you afraid of him?"

"No, that's not my battle to fight."

"Even if he's the one that had your parents killed?"

"It wasn't him. I remember the man that betrayed them."

"Alistair and then King Edwards Chamberlain were the culprits and that's the truth."

"I don't believe you!" She hissed.

"Was the man's name, Ballard?"

Her eyes widened and the look of anger flooded over her face, "How do you know that name?"

"That is the name of the Chamberlain."

"How do I know you're not deceiving me like they did my parents?"

Rowan placed both hands on each side of his helmet and lifted it up revealing his face, "Why would I betray you, Ellyn?"

"Ulrich," she cried out, her voice filled with excitement just to see him once again. "You're the Black Knight? This whole time you helped us and you never told me?"

"I couldn't," he replied. "It would compromise the mission. And I wanted you to see your brother again. Help you the way you helped us back when you didn't have too. And now it's time for me to help you get your revenge."

"Why now?" Ellyn asked. "Back then you hated it when someone spoke ill of your precious King. What changed?"

"I never realised how evil Alistair truly was until now. He kills innocent people at will, sacrifices the Knights Of Valor for his own amusement. All in the name of building his one world order where he would be god. The man is dangerous and needs to be stopped at all cost. Will you help?"

"I can't spare any of the knight's except for Sheana and that will be up to her. Perhaps I know of another who could help us."

"You will help me then?"

"Revenge no longer matters, but stopping a madman does."

"Thank you Ellyn. I will never be able to repay you for what you are about to do."

"You can thank me after we win."

"I will keep that in mind," Ulrich smiled. "If you wouldn't mind I would like you to meet some friends of mine. They want to put an end to King Alistair as well."

"When do you want us to meet them?"

"Two weeks from today.

"Where?"

"Somewhere neutral."

"Perhaps here," she suggested.

"That would work perfectly for everyone."

"Then it's settled."

"Before I leave I just wanted you to know something."

"What?"

"It was nice seeing you again," he said with a smile.

Ellyn could feel the warmth radiating from her face, "You too."

Ulrich after being away for a year or so had finally returned to the Kingdom Of Drasal. Caine was the first to greet him as soon as he entered the castle. He was wearing different armor then what the First Knight should. His hair was longer and pulled back into a ponytail and his eyes seemed more powerful.

"Ulrich, it's good to see you well," Caine responded.

"You as well my friend," Ulrich replied. "How have things been here?"

"Going according to plan. Did you finish your training with Zerius?"

"I did and Zerius said I was ready to claim what is rightfully mine." Ulrich's mind flashed back to the time he spent training with the mage. It was one of the most grueling and intense things he had ever put his body and mind through. Zerius was an extreme man, he had made Ulrich practice the Dark Arts under conditions that would kill the normal person.

Even when he was supposed to meditate that became a dangerous session as well. The most grueling part of his training began when Zerius would summon undead warriors to test Ulrich's ability. He would train for hours on end with the way of the blade. Also learn new ways in the Dark Arts which took a toll on his body at times.

Zerius pushed him to his limits until he was able to fuse magic into his blade and parts of his body with ease. The final test was when Ulrich would be able to test his strength against the mage leader. And the day came when the student bested the teacher. Which pleased Zerius greatly and announced that it was now Ulrich's time to take his place in the history books.

"Did you place the other plan in motion?" Caine asked.

"With ease. What is our next move?"

"First I have to pay some friends a visit."

"You have friends?" Ulrich laughed.

"More like pawns in our little game," Caine smirked.

"Be sure to tell your friends to meet me at Ormkirk. Hearing that we have the backing of the Elite Guard should help us more than anything else would."

"Before we part ways, just a quick question."

Ulrich's brow raised, "Yes?"

"Have you heard anything of Gawain and Leon?"

"Nothing," Ulrich answered. "Though Zerius did sense a spike in power and it vanished as quickly as it came. Honestly I think that was them making their return to these lands."

"Good. This will not work without them."

"If I'm correct I'm sure I will have a run in with them sooner than later."

"Great, let's finish setting the wheels of fate into motion."

For some reason it felt as though Leon was walking the path that he must when he returned to Wespington. He couldn't explain it, he just knew it. It was also nice to see Micha and King Peregrine again even though he wished it was under better circumstances. Gawain was off in the King's throne room with Micha explaining what they were about to embark on.

Leon had hoped that Gawain could convince them to lend their aid in this fight. His former teacher was correct with his words, they had no chance of winning without help. Though it didn't matter to Leon, with or without aid he was going to end Alistair. Regardless of the outcome he did know of someone that would help. Ellyn and the Elite guard would offer assistance in their new quest.

Gawain and Micha returned from the castle and joined Leon and the rest of the group. The two men explained that King Peregrine would offer us aid. Micha and a few hand selected Knight's Of Wespington will come with us and join the battle. Micha stepped in and informed them that he also had supplies. That would help them as well and some fresh horses on top of that.

Gawain also said that King Peregrine was going to allow them to use one of their ships to gather the rest of his men. Then come back to gather Micha and his knights along with the supplies and horses. This would aid them greatly in one of the biggest missions of their lives. And if Aurelius could talk his brethren into aiding them it could tip the balance in their favor.

This time though Leon decided he would stay behind and help Micha get everything ready upon Gawain's return. He thought it was important for Cathrine and Gawain to do this on their own. "What made you stay behind and help me?" Micha questioned Leon.

"They do not need me tagging along," Leon answered.

"Is he not your teacher?" Micha looked confused.

"Once upon a time he was."

"What changed?" Micha asked. Leon didn't want to go into detail, so instead he gave a brief description of what transpired after they had parted ways. "I see," said Micha. "Never thought things would escalate this far."

"That makes two of us."

"Can we even win this battle?"

Leon shrugged, "We can run and let the dice fall where they may. Or we stay and fight with a slight chance of victory, either way Alistair would still try and kill us," he explained.

"After we are done here let's head for the pub."

"Why?"

"To celebrate."

"Celebrate what?"

"Life or death and a small chance of victory," Micha smiled. "Plus we may never get the chance to taste fine mead ever again."

Leon slapped Micha on the back, "Guess we can't have that now can we?" He responded.

On the third day Gawain and crew had returned, Leon remembered there being a lot less mercenaries upon his first visit. Gawain explained that he had done some recruiting and it had gone quite well. Apparently there were more than enough men and women that hated King Alistair for the crimes he has committed.

Leon voiced his concerns but Gawain was quick to point out they didn't have very many options and could not afford to be picky. Gawain also assured him that most of them were warriors and the others could be trained rather quickly. Micha even agreed that he and his men could have them in fighting shape in a couple of days.

"What of Henry and Jeffery?" Leon asked.

"Jeffery is helping with the supplies we brought back. Henry no longer wishes to fight as he said before. Perhaps he is wise in his choice."

"Perhaps," Leon agreed.

"Enough of the small talk," Aurelius interrupted. "I wish to head back to Rehakadi. Allora needs to be updated on all that has transpired, I'm sure she is sick with worry."

"No patience as usual," Gawain sighed.

"Who will be coming along with us?" Leon asked.

"Just the three of us," Aurelius answered. "It will be quicker that way and we will draw less attention towards us."

"What of supplies?"

"Only water and our weapons, we shall hunt for food when needed."

"Why do I feel like you're hiding something from us," said Gawain.

"Just homesick is all my friend."

Gawain studied his friend with a keen eye wishing to question him further. But decided against it, whatever the elven man was hiding he was sure it would come to light before long. Micha was kind enough to offer them Wespington's fastest and strongest steeds. They thanked him kindly as the horses would cut their time in half.

Upon their travels to Hyss woods, the men noticed that something didn't feel right. It was quiet too quiet if you asked them. Usually this part of the land was bustling with life. Knights from neighboring kingdoms would be patrolling the area for bandits. While traveling caravans flooded the area fighting for their next spot to sell their wares.

"This isn't right," Aurelius stated.

"Could be a trap," said Gawain.

Leon rode over to take a paper that was nailed to a tree, "It's worse than we imagined," he muttered as he was joined by Aurelius and Gawain. "Read this." He handed the paper ove.

"Any trader of goods shall be inspected by the Knights Of Valor then placed in a designated area. Half of any gold or silver earned by any and all caravans will be given to King Alistair. Whoever tries to betray the King shall be put to death. We do this in the name of the one world order." Flames erupted from Gawain's hand burning the paper to ash. "Let's keep moving," he grunted.

Not a word was spoken until they were standing at the entrance of Hyss Woods. Or at least what used to be Hyss Woods, what was once a great elven city. Was now nothing more than a pile of rubble. The trees had been destroyed, completely cut down to the roots. And the city was burned beyond recognition. Aurelius fell to his knees and let out a loud cry of disbelief and great pain.

There was nothing that could be said that would help the situation. Nothing that could help with the pain Aurelius had felt over losing his homeland, his family, his friends. Gawain was starting to worry for not only his friend but for their chances of winning this battle. Aurelius was one of the best known elven warriors that could beat damn near anyone. This is the man that trained his warriors in the ways of the blade and magic alike. Allora was also a powerful Elder with unlimited use of earth magic at her disposal. Defeating them would be no easy feet even with the aid of the Dark Ones and yet Alistair had done so.

Aurelius stood with his fists clenched tightly, his body trembled with rage. He silently made a promise to himself that he would avenge his fallen comrades even if it meant his death. He didn't say a word while he climbed back up on the saddle and spurred the horse onward. It was a long quiet ride back to Wespington.

When they made their return the small militia was ready to depart. All they waited for was a leader to step up and lead the way. Aurelius and Gawain discussed who that should be. Both were in agreement that it should be Leon.

Leon was hesitant and didn't want to be responsible for the lives of others. Though this was his mission now and the others had stepped back for that reason. Like it or not he had to accept his destiny that it was time for him to lead. Time to see if he can make a difference in these dark times.

"One last stop before we make our stand," said Leon.

"And that is?" Gawain asked.

"Ormkirk," Leon answered. "There is a strong feeling telling me we have to go there before we engage the enemy."

"As you wish." Gawain bowed.

Leon was taken back by Gawain's response, his former teacher didn't even put up a fight. And Aurelius didn't offer his opinion either all he said was that he would take up the end. Probably still needed some time to himself to figure things out. Micha walked up before they departed with some new armor for him to wear.

"What is this?" Leon questioned.

"Armor for the man in charge," Micha replied. "A captain needs to stand out."

"Thank you," Leon said, accepting the gift kindly.

There it was the great city of Ormkirk, it was a sight to behold. It was always said that Drasal was the largest of all cities. But after beholding the great city for the first time. Ormkirk was actually greater than where he once trained and called home. Though there was no time to enjoy the city and take in the sights. They needed to get to the castle and ask to speak with Ellyn.

What they didn't expect when they had gotten there was the group of what could only be explained as outsiders waiting around outside. "What do you think they are doing here?" Aurelius asked.

"If I had to guess the same reason we are here," Gawain answered.

"What makes you say that?" replied Leon.

"They are a fairly decent size resistance group led by a man that goes by the name Stilfadr. He approached me a while back and asked me if I could aid him."

"What did he need help with?"

"He wanted to take down King Aidan and wanted to enlist my help."

"And?"

"I refused."

"Why?"

"At the time I thought it was a fool's errand."

"More than likely it was," Leon replied. "Time to see if Ellyn has time to visit with us." As they approached the large wooden doors opened. Out came Ellyn with the captain of the guard but he couldn't remember her name. There was also a very muscular man dressed like a woodsman walking with them as well. Along with another wearing all black armor and a red cape.

Ellyn caught a glimpse of them out of the corner of her eye. She turned and made her way over to greet her friends. That she hadn't seen in such a long time. Ulrich was right, it was only a matter of time before they were all reunited once again.

"Princess Ellyn," Gawain bowed.

Ellyn waved him off, "We're friends there is no need to bow to me," she said. "What are you guys doing here?"

"We need your help," Leon answered.

"Does this have anything to do with Alistair?" She asked.

"As a matter of fact it does," he responded. "Am I guessing we're late for the party?"

"It would seem the day of reckoning is upon us."

"How did Stilfadr get involved in this?" Gawain asked.

"He said a man named Shawn asked him to come here and give me this." Ellyn handed over a rolled up parchment paper to Gawain. "Stilfadr also explained that Alistair was an evil man that had already taken lives and burned kingdoms to the ground. He wishes to help us put an end to him."

"These are blueprints to the Castle Of Drasal," Gawain gasped.

"That it is," Ellyn replied. "Supposedly Shawn was hired to steal the papers and hand them over to Stilfadr."

"In exchange for your support," Gawain said with a hint of sarcasm.

"That's not true, I was going to aid them regardless."

"Why would you do that?" Questioned Leon.

"Because of him." Ellyn pointed at the Black Knight.

"This has nothing to do with him," Leon snapped.

"It has everything to do with him," said Ellyn.

"Hello old friend." The knight removed his helmet showing his face.

"Ulrich," Leon hissed unsheathing his blade.

Gawain drew upon Ulrich as well, "What in the hell are you doing here?" He spate.

Ulrich laughed at the notion of trying to pick a fight with them at this time. "There is no need for hostility," he said. "I am here as a friend not as your enemy."

"I demand you put your swords away!" Shena shouted. "If the Princess says he's a friend then that is the way it shall be." Gawain and Leon reluctantly sheathed their blades. "Good that we have an understanding."

"Look guys, I know you hate me and I don't blame you," Ulrich began. "I apologize for the things I have done to you both. Especially you Gawain, you warned me about Alistair and Caine and I did not listen. And I even turned my back on my best friend for that Leon, I am truly sorry. Both Alistair and Caine are mad for power. Both want to build a one world order. I've seen the horrible things they have done to get what they want."

"We're supposed to trust you?" Leon replied.

"No," he answered. "All I ask is that you let me help you end this. After that let the chips fall where they may."

"Do we have a choice?" Gawain grunted.

"Not if you want our aid," Shena interrupted.

"Please one last fight. All of us together to end this once and for all," Ellyn pleaded.

She had put them on the spot turning the tables asking for her friends to fight beside her one last time. Reluctantly they had agreed but not without making a promise that after the battle Ulrich would be confronted. Not only that, they both made sure to let him know he wasn't trusted. All had come together under the same banner and ready to take the fight to Alistair.

What was once a small militia had turned into a full blown army with some of the best kingdoms had to offer. And being led by the chosen one they had a slime chance of victory. The war march was on and the army carried two different flags held high in the air. One was the flag of the Academy Of Drasal and the other was the flag of Rehakadi. It was to honor and avenge their fallen comrades.

A guard on lookout yelled out that an army was on its way. And started ringing a bell alerting everyone danger was on the way.

Another man shouted for the drawbridge to be raised. But the crazed King Alistair demanded his horse be brought to him and the drawbridge be left down.

He also demanded that Caine gather the Knights Of Valor and he would summon the Dark Ones and meet their guests on the battlefield. Caine on knowing who was marching towards them threw on a helmet to hide his identity. In Alistair's twisted mind this was going to be fun, he had been bored as of late.

Alistair laughed when he met the ragtag army before him on the battlefield. "Look who it is," he said. "Gawain, and his former student Leon." He looked over at Aurelius, "Oh and the last surviving Elven man from Rehakadi is here as well. I will enjoy killing you like I did your brothers."

"You will die here today that is the promise I make!" Aurelius angrily shouted.

"Bold words," Alistair responded. "For your sake they had better be true or your people die with you." That's when he noticed Ulrich riding with the enemy. "You are against me as well?" He hissed.

"Your time as King is over," Ulrich said.

"King?" He laughed. "I am a God!"

"Even a God can be killed!" Ulrich barked back.

"I'm going to enjoy watching all of you die," said Alistair. "Prepare yourself men!"

Leon raised his blade into the air, "The time to fight is now! This is our one and only chance to vanquish evil here and now! We will win the day here on this very battlefield!" He shouted.

"Show them no mercy," Alistair demanded. "This is the very last hurdle we must overcome! To create a one world order of peace for all that deserve and fight for it!" Alistair unsheathed the Reaper Blade and pointed it at the resistance, "Attack!"

"We end this!" Leon shouted spurring his horse onward.

And another great battle took place, it would be a battle that would change the world of Todrain forever. Swords clashed and steel met steel as the war waged on. Leon was reluctant at first to harm any

Knight Of Valor as was Gawain. Until they had realized how badly their minds had been poisoned by Alistair they didn't have a choice.

Aurelius on the other hand had no such qualms and was shedding blood like a man possessed. He cast spell after spell tore through flesh with his blade. With one thought in mind, getting his hands on Alistair and gaining his vengeance.

Gawain and Leon fought bravely as well with Ulrich oddly being on their side. Jeffrey aided in the fight as Cathrine tended to the wounded, even helping the Knights Of Valor that laid down their swords. Stilfadr proved his prowess. Taking down any man that drew upon him with his trusted hatchet and small blade in hand.

Alistair sat back and watched the battle unfold, he had seen no reason to participate unless necessary. He thought his Knights Of Valor would lead them to victory. But the men had been worn out from the lack of rest on his conquest of dominance.

"Do you not fight my King?" Caine questioned. "The men could use the help of their God."

"Why do you not fight?" Alistair turned to Caine and asked.

"I was hoping to see your godly powers in action," he mockingly replied.

"The Dark Ones will take care of this," Alistair spate. "No need to get my hands dirty."

"Then let's see it."

"Dark Ones, this is your master speaking. Destroy the ones that would defy your God," he demanded. The Dark Knights listened, making their presence known on the battlefield. They mowed down the resistance like they were nothing. Skilled warriors were no match for them and dropped like flies.

Unfortunately Jeffrey tried and failed at trying to battle against them. He fought valiantly but his skills were no match for that of the Dark Knights. The tip of the Dark Ones blade ripped through Jeffrey's armor and pierced his lung. Leon witnessed what had happened and rushed to aid his friend. He disposed of the Dark Knight before kneeling down to check on Jeffrey.

Jeffrey was coughing up blood as Leon called for help until Cathrine heard his cries and rushed over. She tried desperately to heal him but the wound was fatal there was nothing she could do for him. "Save him!" Leon shouted.

Tears formed in the corner of her eyes, "There's nothing I can do," she replied. "I'm sorry."

"I don't believe you!"

"I'm so sorry." She kept repeating herself.

Jeffrey reached up and grabbed Leon's wrist, "Leon, promise that you will finish this," he said.

"We have to help you first."

"Promise me," Jeffrey pleaded.

"I promise," said Leon. Jeffrey's grip loosened and his hand fell to the ground. "Jeffrey wake up." He shook him and pleaded over and over again for him to open his eyes.

Cathrine placed her hand on Leon's shoulder, "He's gone she said," she told him.

Leon stayed on his knees with his head lowered, his will to fight was no longer there. One of the Dark Knights had his blade lifted and swiftly brought it down. The evil being was about to kill Cathrine and Leon with one foul swoop. Ulrich at the last second blocked the attack saving them both. He quickly fused his blade with magic and swung the sword upward tearing the Dark One appart.

Ulrich pulled Leon to his feet, "What in the hell are you doing?" He shouted. "Pull yourself together or Alistair wins. Is that what you want?"

"Why bother?"

Ulrich slapped him across the face, "These people are fighting and dying for you. Gawain and Ellyn are fighting for you! Are you just going to let them die as well?"

"I don't know what to do," Leon muttered.

"Let that power of yours erupt. Stop fighting it!" Blue flames formed around Leon's body. As he focused his anger and rage allowing it to flow through his veins. "You ready to take these guys down?"

"What do you suggest?" Leon questioned.

"The ring of fire."

"That will drain us," Leon replied.

"It will win the day and send that coward running," Ulrich said. "Then we can finish him in the castle that way no one else will get hurt."

"Let's do it," Leon smirked.

"Been a while. Do you still remember how?"

"Of course."

"Let's hope so or we both get burned to a crisp."

Leon didn't make a response, instead he focused on enveloping his body with the fire spell. Not many people could pull this off but Ulrich worked with him until the technique was perfected. Ulrich did the same and both their bodies exploded with fire. Both were emitting enough power that the ground began to shake.

"Is this the ring of fire they had talked about so many years ago?" Gawain muttered. His eyes widened as he realized what was about to transpire. "Everyone get down!" He screamed out loud.

"Here we go," Caine talked under his breath. "This should be fun."

Leon sprinted ahead with Ulrich right behind him. Then it was like they had become one. All that could be seen was the Dark Knights falling to the ground in flames. The two young men's speed was fast enough that they could not be seen by the normal eye.

"What insanity is this?" Alistair said with a look of fear on his face.

"A power that was taught to them a long time ago," Caine replied with a smug look on his face. "The Dark Knights have been defeated. What now God Alistair?"

"Retreat."

"What was that?"

"Retreat!" Alistair pulled the reins of his horse and spurred it on in the direction of Drasal. Caine disappeared into the shadows not following Alistair back to the castle.

The remaining survivors of the resistance cheered when they witnessed Alistair fleeing the battlefield. The Dark Ones had been defeated and the rest of the Knights Of Valor bowed down to the victors. They believed the day was won and evil had been dethroned. Though Aurelius, Gawain, Leon and Ulrich knew better. It would never be over until Alistair had been dealt with once and for all.

"Now what?" Leon huffed and puffed clearly weakened from the technique he and Ulrich used.

"We use the blueprints and get inside the castle and finish this," Gawain answered.

"Agreed," said Ulrich.

Aurelius, Ellyn, Gawain, Leon and Ulrich had decided it all started with them and would end with them. Cathrine and Stilfadr were asked to stay behind and tend to the wounded and watch the enemy. Both voiced their objections but it fell on deaf ears.

The group of five followed the blueprints exactly. Leading them through an underground cavern that was underneath Drasal. It led them up through the dungeons and inside the castle. Caine stuck to the plan and made sure there were no guards in wait. He also had double checked that the doors to the throne room were left unlocked.

"Do you think they pursued us?" Alistair questioned.

Caine shrugged, "Not sure?" he replied. "Arc you afraid?"

"Gods are afraid of nothing. Though that power does have me concerned."

"So it should." Caine slowly walked towards the large double doors.

"What are you doing?" Alistair gasped.

"Putting an end to this," Caine responded as he opened the doors. "Hope your godly powers are enough to save you."

"You dare betray your King and God!" Alistair angrily shouted.

Caine laughed, "Do you really think that I was doing all of this for your one world kingdom? If so you really are foolish."

"We are brothers in arms. Set to build a brand new world."

"No Alistair, you were nothing more than another pawn in my game."

The group of hero's rushed inside the throne room, not realising Caine was standing off in the shadows. This was it, this was the final battle or so they had thought. "Put the Reaper Blade on the ground and surrender. It's over Alistair you've lost this fight," said Gawain.

"Or fight us and my blade will taste your flesh," Aurelius added. "Either way you're not leaving here alive."

Alistair shook his head and sighed, "Do you think it will be that easy?" He smirked, "What if I told you that I am no longer the man you think I am. That Alistair decided to give himself to the blade and I am what took over."

"The essence of Cromwell," Leon said.

"Ah, you must be the Chosen One. But not the one I'm looking for, though he is here."

"Shut up and fight!" Ulrich belted out loud.

"I see," Alistair or Cromwell responded.

"Take him down," Gawain commanded. "If he retreated here then he has weakened."

"Quite the opposite. Now that I am in full control over this pathetic man my power has grown. And it's all thanks to you."

"It won't last," Gawain replied. "The body will deteriorate before long."

"It will last long enough to kill the lot of you." Alistair's body started to glow an intense dark purple. His face distorted and his body mass increased. He let out a loud ungodly howl as his powers erupted throughout the castle. When he looked back at them his eyes had become dark and soulless. "Once I am done I will finally become one with my vessel and become whole once again," he announced.

"Not if we send you back to hell!" Leon screamed out.

"Alright then, lets see what you've got chosen one."

Leon darted forward raising his blade for an attack, when their blades collided a powerful explosion filled the room. Knocking all back except for Ulrich. Caine rushed past handing Ulrich the jewel of power that the Chamberlain had acquired months ago.

Ulrich crushed the jewel allowing its power to flow through his veins and mixing with his own. He quickly jumped in to help Leon fight against Cromwell. Cromwell was strong enough to knock Leon and Ulrich back. Leon went in for another attack but was knocked to the ground, he barely rolled out of the away before Cromwell could stab him.

Ulrich lunged through the air bringing his sword down at Cromwell's head but was thrown into a wall for his effort. He lay on the ground trying to figure out what he was doing wrong. With the powers Zerius bestowed upon him along with the power of the jewel, he should be strong enough to finish this.

Leon was ready to go on the offensive again when he heard his father's voice. "Stop holding back," his father told him. "Let it all go, like you did in the tomb. If you don't everyone you love will die." The young man felt as though he had enough power in him for one last finale attack. The blue aura surrounded him again, this time he was in control of the power.

He focused it all into the blade, if he was correct it should be enough to wound Cromwell's newly acquired body. He rushed towards Cromwell again bringing the blade upward in a slashing motion. It broke the barrier and cut through Cromwell's armor causing a large wound to his chest.

"You little shit!" Cromwell bellowed. "I will kill you for that!"

Ulrich stood and let his power flow through him as well, this was his last chance and took advantage. He quickly darted forward and with Cromwell's guard dropped he plunged his blade into his back. Cromwell looked over his shoulder at Ulrich, "Damn it," he spate. "I'm going to make you both pay for this."

"I don't think so," Ulrich whispered. "I am your supposed vessel."

"What?" Cromwell's eyes widened.

"And guess what else," Ulrich said. "I have the power to reject you and I do so. Before I send you back to Hades know your power will be of great use to me."

Leon ran his blade through him again, "Go back to hell you monster!" He shouted and stabbed him again. Ulrich ran his blade through Cromwell's back again and again. In the end he grabbed the Reaper Blade from Cromwell's hands and lopped off his head. Leon was weakened and fell to his knees gasping for air. "Thank the gods it's over," he said. "Now we need to destroy that damn blade along with this one as planned."

Ulrich remembered what Zerius had told him. When the fight was over, he needed to claim the blade and Cromwell's power for his own. He took the Reaper Blade and plunged it into the headless corpse. That power was absorbed into the blade and flowed into Ulrich's body. Giving him a sense of strength he had never felt before.

"Destroy the blade," Leon pleaded with his friend.

"Sorry Leon that's not part of the plan," Ulrich responded.

"What are you talking about?"

Gawain slowly walked up, hobbling on his right leg, "He used us."

"Smart as always old man," Ulrich smirked.

"Is that true?" Leon questioned.

"Who do you think planned all of this?"

"What about my parents? Was that a lie?" Ellyn questioned with a look of sadness in her eyes.

"Alistair had nothing to do with that," Caine said stepping out of the shadows. "That was all me."

"You bastards!" Ellyn spate.

Ulrich walked over to her, "There is one last thing I must do," he said.

"Haven't you done enough," Ellyn cried. "I loved you Ulrich."

"You walked away from me. I gave you a chance and you refused me. But I will fix that." He plunged the Reaper Blade into her chest.

"I'm sorry Ellyn, but you're my weakness and I can't have that. You were the last hurdle that stood in my way."

"No!" Both Gawain and Leon shouted.

Gawain went to draw upon Ulrich but his leg gave out on him and he fell on the floor. "When will you learn to just give up," Caine smirked putting the tip of his blade to Gawain's throat.

"What are you waiting for?" Gawain shouted. "Finish me off you coward!"

Leon went to help Ellyn and was forced against the wall by Ulrich's new found powers, "Stay put."

"I'm not going to kill you Gawain," said Caine. "I want you to live with the fact that I used you once again. You have failed and people will die because of you. When will you understand that you can never beat me?"

"I swear if you don't kill me now, I will kill you someday," Gawain spate.

"Perhaps," Caine replied. "But not on this day."

"Leon." Ulrich lowered his hand releasing the spell that had him pinned against the wall. "Join me," he said. "With our combined powers imagine the things we can accomplish together."

"You lead us to believe you had finally come to your senses. Yet you betrayed us again and killed Ellyn! How dare you ask me to join you! I would rather kill you!"

"That hurts my feelings."

"You have no feelings left!"

"I give you one last chance to join me."

"Or what? Are you going to kill me like you did Ellyn?"

"I should." Ulrich held up the Reaper Blade, "Though I doubt you will even be a threat to me." He swung the blade through the air making some type of portal in space and time. "Let us go Caine. We have work to do." He looked back at Leon, "Stay away," he warned. "Or next time I will take everything you hold dear to your heart."

"Looks like playtime is over. Give Cathrine a kiss for me," Caine smiled.

"You son of a bitch!" Gawain yelled trying to get to his feet. But by that time Caine and Ulrich had walked through the portal and disappeared with the exit closing behind them. "Leon! We need to give chase!" Gawain bellowed.

"It's too late," Leon muttered. "They're gone." He stared down at the lifeless body of Ellyn. He fought against the urge to cry but he needed to be strong for the time being. Leon knelt down and scooped her body in his arms. "I'm sorry that I couldn't protect you," he whispered.

"Use your powers the way Ulrich did," Gawain demanded. "We have to go after them."

"No," Leon recoiled. "I don't give a damn about them right now. Ellyn deserves a hero's burial and that's what she will get." He started out of the castle not caring if Gawain was following or not. Cheers erupted when the castle doors had opened. But when they had seen Gawain stager out behind Leon carrying Ellyn's body all went quiet.

Shena went running up to them as Leon knelt down placing her body on the ground. The Captain Of The Guard shook Ellyn's body demanding that she wake up. She cried and cried pleading for the princess to wake but she was already gone. Lance pulled her away and consoled the crying captain in his arms.

A few days later a funeral was held in honor of Ellyn and Jeffrey and all others that had fallen in battle. Queen Mina and Prince Riu both gave speeches of their sisters bravery. Saying how she had always been the tough one even in the face of danger. Shena was next to speak, she had known Ellyn better than anyone. She was the one that trained her to fight, and also taught her how to care for others when no one else would.

Shena sobbed as she spoke further of whom she considered not only a friend but a daughter. The townspeople cried for the loss of another royal family member. Lance and his men were there to, too pay their respects as well. Gawain was there leaning on his cane for support with Cathrine standing by his side holding his hand.

Aurelius was there as well, as a show of respect for such a great person and warrior.

As the ceremony was coming to an end. The small boats that they placed Ellyn and Jeffrey's bodies on and decorated. Was pushed out to sea while music was being played. The Knights Of Ormkirk were shooting flaming arrows towards the boats setting them ablaze. It was the final step in allowing their spirits to enter Valhalla.

Leon watched it all take place from afar he did not wish to make his presence known. Once the ceremony was over he mounted his horse and rode away, disappearing off in the distance. Leaving all he had ever known and cared for behind him.

"What are we doing here?" Caine questioned.

"Do you not remember this place?" Ulrich replied.

"I do," Caine answered. "This was once a great city and where I found you so long ago."

"Then you should know why we are here."

"Do tell."

"This will be a great city once again where only the strong will be welcomed."

"So this is where we will build it?"

Ulrich nodded, "Go now Caine round up those filthy peasants and bring them here to start building our new kingdom."

"If they refuse?"

"Kill them."

Caine bowed, "As you wish my one and only true King."

THE END

Dear reader,

We hope you enjoyed reading *Shadow of a Traitor*. Please take a moment to leave a review, even if it's a short one. Your opinion is important to us.

Discover more books by A.E. Stanfill at https://www.nextchapter.pub/authors/ae-stanfill

Want to know when one of our books is free or discounted? Join the newsletter at http://eepurl.com/bqqB3H

Best regards,

A.E. Stanfill and the Next Chapter Team

Lightning Source UK Ltd.
Milton Keynes UK
UKHW041841021120
372685UK00001B/99